Hadn't Kyle said he would give her anything?

"All you have to do is ask," he'd said.

What if she came right out and asked him to impregnate her?

Afterward, the child would be hers to raise. She would neither expect nor demand anything further of Kyle.

It could work!

Rebecca's excitement built. Yes, yes, it definitely could work. After all, she was a grown woman, not a teenager. She was educated. She had a good income. And she had a lot of family support. She could give a child a full, good life.

Kyle's baby.

A part of her beloved that would belong to her forever.

And all Rebecca had to do…

…was ask.

Dear Reader,

It's that joyful time of year again! And Santa has some wonderfully festive books coming your way this December.

Bestselling author Marie Ferrarella brings you our THAT'S MY BABY! for December. This holiday bundle of joy is still a secret to his or her dad…and Mom is sure to be a *Christmas Bride*.

And the patter of little feet doesn't stop there. Don't miss *A Baby for Rebecca* by Trisha Alexander, the latest in her THREE BRIDES AND A BABY miniseries. *Holly and Mistletoe* is Susan Mallery's newest title in the HOMETOWN HEARTBREAKERS miniseries, a tale filled with Christmas warmth and love. And for those of you who've been enjoying Tracy Sinclair's CUPID'S LITTLE HELPERS miniseries, this month we've got *Mandy Meets a Millionaire*—with the help of some little matchmakers.

December also brings Diana Whitney's *Barefoot Bride*—the heroine is an amnesiac woman in a wedding dress who finds love with a single dad and his kids at Christmastime. This is the second book in Diana's wonderful PARENTHOOD miniseries. *The Sheriff's Proposal* by Karen Rose Smith is a warm, tender tale that takes place during the season of giving.

I hope you enjoy all our books this month. All of us here at Silhouette wish you a happy, healthy holiday season!

Sincerely,

Tara Gavin
Senior Editor

Please address questions and book requests to:
Silhouette Reader Service
U.S.: 3010 Walden Ave., P.O. Box 1325, Buffalo, NY 14269
Canadian: P.O. Box 609, Fort Erie, Ont. L2A 5X3

TRISHA ALEXANDER

A BABY FOR REBECCA

SPECIAL EDITION®

Published by Silhouette Books
America's Publisher of Contemporary Romance

This book is dedicated to Julie Kistler, who gave me the idea. Thanks, Julie. I owe you one!
Special thanks to the best writing buddies on earth:
Heather MacAllister and her alter ego Heather Allison, Kay David, Alaina Hawthorne and Amanda Stevens.

 SILHOUETTE BOOKS

ISBN 0-373-24070-8

A BABY FOR REBECCA

Copyright © 1996 by Patricia A. Kay

Printed in U.S.A.

TRISHA ALEXANDER

has had a lifelong love affair with books and has always wanted to be a writer. She also loves cats, movies, the ocean, music, Broadway shows, cooking, traveling, being with her family and friends, Cajun food, "Calvin and Hobbes" and getting mail. Trisha and her husband have three grown children, three adorable grandchildren and live in Houston, Texas. Trisha loves to hear from readers. You can write to her at P.O. Box 441603, Houston, TX 77244-1603.

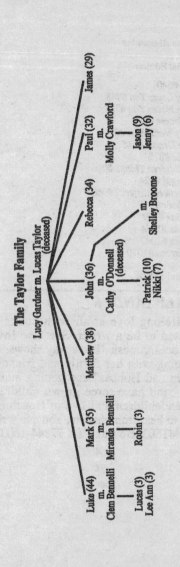

The Taylor Family

Lucy Gardner m. Lucas Taylor
(deceased)

Luke (44)
m.
Clem Bennelli

Mark (35)
m.
Miranda Bennelli

Matthew (38)

John (36)
m.
Cathy O'Donnell
(deceased)

Rebecca (34)

Paul (32)
m.
Molly Crawford

James (29)

Lucas (3)
Lee Ann (3)

Robin (3)

Patrick (10)
Nikki (7)

m.
Shelley Broome

Jason (9)
Jenny (6)

Prologue

From the pages of The Cleveland Plain Dealer

Woman Receives Citation For Bravery
by Rose Janson

Yesterday afternoon, in a ceremony at City Hall, Fire Chief Ronald Delatorrio presented the Cleveland Fire Department Citation for Bravery to thirty-two-year-old Rebecca Elaine Taylor of Chagrin Falls. At approximately 10:00 p.m. last August 14, while working late at the offices of Alonzo & Christopher, the advertising agency where she is employed as an account representative, Ms. Taylor became aware of the smell of smoke. In investigating its source, she realized there was a rapidly spreading fire in progress. Unable to reach the fire-alarm box, she dialed the emergency number and alerted officials; then, remembering that she had seen a co-worker in the building earlier, she fought her way to his office to make sure he was safely gone. There she found him asleep. After awakening him and warning him of the danger, they crawled their way to the stairway and eventually made it safely to the ground floor of the building. Ms. Taylor and her colleague, Kyle G. MacNeill, grandson of Graham D. MacNeill, founder of the MacNeill Department Store chain, suffered from smoke inhalation and minor burns and were hospitalized overnight.

In presenting the framed citation to Ms. Taylor, Chief Delatorrio gave a brief history of the award, then said Ms. Taylor had been chosen to receive it "for her courage, selflessness and quick thinking in the face of grave danger."

Ms. Taylor said she hadn't done anything special. "Anyone would have done the same." She added, "I'm a bit embarrassed, but still thrilled and honored to be given this award. It's going to occupy a place of honor in my office."

When asked for his comments regarding Ms. Taylor's actions, Mr. MacNeill said, "I can never repay her. She saved my life. I'd been working on a new campaign around the clock for days, and I was exhausted. I never smelled the smoke, never realized anything was wrong. If she hadn't checked on me, I wouldn't be here today. I'll never forget it."

Graham MacNeill, in a rare public appearance

since his health has deteriorated, attended the ceremony and added his comments to his grandson's, saying, "Ms. Taylor is a remarkable young woman, and our family will be forever in her debt."

After the presentation, Mayor and Mrs. Filburn hosted a reception in Ms. Taylor's honor.

Chapter One

Two years later...

Rebecca Taylor stood at her sixteenth-floor office window and looked down. Far below, pedestrians hurried along Superior Avenue, bodies bowed as they fought their way against the icy wind coming in off Lake Erie and the steadily worsening snowfall that had begun in the predawn hours.

It was hard to believe that only days ago, she'd been in Houston, enjoying sunny skies and sixty-degree temperatures. And yet, Rebecca didn't regret her decision to move to Cleveland two and a half years ago. In fact, she now preferred the climate in northern Ohio.

Her family thought she was crazy. Well, maybe she was. She only knew that since discovering the joys of four distinct seasons, she wouldn't have it any other way.

Besides, Cleveland held numerous other attractions. A job she loved, for one thing. Freedom from her family's hovering, for another. And then, of course, there was...

"Hey, gorgeous! Welcome back! How were your holidays?" said a teasing, masculine voice, putting an abrupt end to her musings.

Rebecca slowly turned.

Leaning lazily against her open doorway was Cleveland's most important attraction of all—one Kyle Graham MacNeill, the man whose life she'd saved one fateful August night, the man she had been secretly in love with for almost two years.

"Wonderful. How about yours?" As always, her expression revealed nothing but the normal pleasure one would feel upon seeing a co-worker one liked. It betrayed none of her inner emotions—not the involuntary leap of her heart nor the increased speed of her pulse nor the sheer joy that the sight of Kyle always produced.

"About what I expected." He walked into the office and plopped into one of the two navy leather chairs flanking her desk, stretching his long legs out in front of him.

He looked terrific as usual: razor-cut dark brown hair just tousled enough to keep it from looking too perfect; skin lightly tanned from a recent golfing vacation in Palm Springs; beautifully designed charcoal suit and pale blue shirt. Even now, slouched comfortably, he looked the very picture of good health and success. The kind of man you might see pictured in *Gentleman's Quarterly.* The kind of man whose charm was effortless and completely ingrained. The kind of man who could have his pick of beautiful women ... and did.

"Is that good or bad?" Rebecca said, shaking off the depressing thought that she was not beautiful and never would be.

He gave her a cynical smile. "What do you think?"

"Bad?"

"It sure wasn't peace on earth, goodwill toward men. What a family I've got! Kevin bitching about Abigail the entire time, Dad bitching about Mom the entire time, and poor Gramps. He was sick. Fighting a bad case of bronchitis."

"Oh, I'm sorry."

He shrugged. "Like I said, what I expected."

"What about your grandfather? Is he still sick?"

Now his expression changed, his blue eyes filling with warmth, his smile genuine. "No. I talked to him this morning, and he's feeling much better. He's a tough old bird." This last was said with pride.

"I'm glad." Rebecca knew how much Kyle's grandfather meant to him. Although Kyle normally affected a got-the-world-by-its-tail persona, he had once confided to Rebecca that his grandfather was the only person he had ever been able to count on.

"So tell me about Houston," he said. "Did the entire clan gather? Did your sister-in-law make it?"

"Yes, everyone made it. We were kind of worried about Clem and Luke—we weren't sure she would be finished with her assignment in Manila—but they turned up on Christmas Eve. You should have seen them. They were lugging all of Luke's photography equipment because they hadn't had time to ship it home to Chicago. Plus they had all these Christmas presents for everyone. And then, of course, they have the twins, who go everywhere they go."

Mentioning her brother's adorable two-year-olds reminded Rebecca of the aching emptiness and envy she'd experienced when she'd watched Luke and Clem with little Lee Ann and Lucas.

Not that she begrudged her brother and his wife their happiness. Of course she didn't. She was thrilled for them. It was just that she wanted the same things: a husband and a child.

A family of her own.

Unfortunately, since she'd picked such an unlikely prospect to fall in love with, those goals seemed farther away than ever.

And somehow, this Christmas, surrounded by her large family—her brothers and their wives and their children—Rebecca had realized her time was running out. In June she would be thirty-five years old. That old biological clock was ticking furiously.

If she were ever going to have the family she so desperately wanted, she was going to have to do something about it . . . and soon.

"Why so pensive?" Kyle said. "Did something happen in Houston?"

Rebecca could have kicked herself. Sometimes she forgot that all that boyish charm Kyle displayed masked sharply honed instincts and a high degree of intelligence. "No, of course not. It was a wonderful visit. I guess I was just daydreaming. Thinking about the twins and how cute they are."

Kyle smiled and nodded, but Rebecca knew he wasn't really interested. Once, early in their relationship, when the two of them were on their way to a client's office, they'd passed a nursery school where there were dozens of toddlers at play, and Rebecca had exclaimed over how sweet they were. She'd never forget Kyle's comment.

He'd shrugged. "Yeah, well, to each his own. I'm not crazy about little kids."

"Oh," she'd said, "you'll change your mind when you have one of your own. There are a lot of men who think they don't like children but when they get mar—"

He'd cut her off, saying, "That won't happen to me, because I don't intend to get married."

That comment, coming as it did when Rebecca was in the first stages of falling in love with Kyle, had been a cold dose of reality.

Then he'd laughed and reached over to pat her knee. "I'd rather just play the field." His eyes twinkled, and his smile was devilish and pure Kyle. "After we're finished at Carrollton's, what do you say we go to my place? I'll show you my etchings."

Rebecca swatted his hand away. Her response was carefully framed in the same bantering tone. "Behave yourself.'' She had been making similar responses for months, because Kyle was an incorrigible flirt.

Rebecca's co-worker and best friend, JoBeth Weaver, had warned her about him. "Don't make the mistake of taking him seriously," she'd said. "He's totally charming, of course, tons of fun and is genuinely thoughtful and interested in people, so women are constantly falling for him. But he's not the settling-down kind at all. If you make the mistake of thinking you'll be the one to change him, you're just asking to get your heart broken. Believe me, I've seen it happen dozens of times."

Too bad Rebecca hadn't paid attention to JoBeth's advice.

No, that wasn't true.

She *had* paid attention, she just hadn't been able to help herself. After she'd saved his life—just two weeks after starting to work at the agency—he'd been so nice.

He'd sent her flowers and taken her to dinner at the Ritz Carlton's Riverview Room.

Then he'd taken to dropping by her office at the start of each day to share a cup of coffee, a ritual that had continued and become something she looked forward to each morning.

But most importantly of all, he'd taken her under his wing at the agency and shown her the ropes. He'd even requested her as an assistant on his biggest account.

No.

Rebecca hadn't had a chance.

All the attention, all the nice things he'd done, combined with his lethal charm, good looks and genuine wish to be friends, had done its job, and within weeks she was totally in love.

And that love had only grown stronger.

She loved him so much that sometimes it was all she could do to keep it hidden. But she'd done it. She'd had to. For if Kyle were to suspect her feelings, her situation at the agency would be untenable.

"I'd better shove off," Kyle said now, looking at his watch. "I've got a meeting with Mark at ten."

"Oh? Problems?" Mark Alonzo was a partner and their boss, head of the Cleveland branch of the agency.

"No, I think he wants to talk strategy for the Oliver-Berg presentation." Kyle stood, giving her a smile and an offhand wave. "See you later."

Mark Alonzo looked up at Kyle's knock. "Come on in, Kyle. Shut the door behind you, will you?"

What was going on? Kyle wondered, even as he complied with the request. Mark had an open-door policy. The only time Kyle could remember his boss's door being shut was during reviews or reprimands.

For a fleeting moment, he wondered if he'd done anything to raise Mark's ire. Just as quickly as the question formed, Kyle dismissed it. If anything, he had done a superior job for the past months. Ever since coming to work for Alonzo & Christopher, as a matter of fact.

"You did an outstanding job on the Kirshner campaign," Mark said, echoing Kyle's thoughts. "Old man Kirshner himself called me last week to say how pleased he was."

Kyle grinned. "Thanks." Mark's personal management style of always complimenting his employees on a job well done was only one of the reasons Kyle liked the other man so much. The other was that Mark was fair and impartial, not to mention had one of the shrewdest minds in the advertising business today.

Mark leaned forward, dark eyes reflecting some emotion Kyle couldn't identify. "Simon and I have been talking."

Kyle's inner radar sprang to attention. Simon Christopher was the other partner, based in Houston.

"We think it's time for the agency to branch out even further." Mark paused, tenting his hands and studying Kyle thoughtfully. "So we've decided to open a Los Angeles office."

"Oh?"

For the first time since Kyle had entered his office, Mark smiled. The smile transformed his narrow face, making him look almost handsome. "And we want you to manage it."

Kyle's mouth dropped open.

"You look surprised."

"I am."

"Why are you surprised? That we're opening another office...or that we're asking you to head it up?"

Kyle grinned. "Both, I guess."

"I know you need more information about the time frame and salary and responsibilities and all that, but what's your gut feeling? Are you interested?"

"I…" Kyle stopped. *Was* he interested? He thought about palm trees and the ocean and the beautiful weather. Through the window behind Mark, he could see the gray skies and falling snow. No more snow. No more slush. No more gloves and boots and heavy coats. And he would be in charge of a branch office in a new territory. Just the thought of the challenge of competing in the West Coast market started his adrenaline pumping. He met Mark's gaze. "Yes, I'm interested."

Mark's smile expanded. "I had a feeling you'd say that. Okay, here's the deal…"

Some of Kyle's excitement paled as he thought about breaking the news of his upcoming transfer to his grandfather. It would be hard to leave the old man, and yet Kyle knew his grandfather would want him to seize this opportunity. Even though Graham Mac-Neill had been bitterly disappointed when Kyle had shown no interest in entering the family's business, he was proud of Kyle's accomplishments now. "By God," he'd said just a few weeks ago, "you've got guts. You're just like me!"

Kyle wished it were true, but he knew he had a long way to go before he would be just like his grandfather. He admired the old man tremendously. Graham hadn't been born with a silver spoon in his mouth as Kyle had. His education had barely included graduating from high school, whereas Kyle had graduated from Yale and gone on to get his M.B.A. from Northwestern.

But it pleased Kyle that his grandfather thought so highly of him. He had vowed long ago he would never do anything to embarrass or hurt the old man, and that promise to himself had only been reinforced with the latest family fiasco.

Remembering the ugliness of his parents' ongoing divorce dispute and the horrendous breakup his brother, Kevin, had had with his wife—a battle that had disclosed some extremely unsavory details of Kevin's profligate life-style—Kyle couldn't help thinking how disappointed his grandfather must be. Too bad the old man couldn't have had a family like Rebecca's.

Rebecca.

Kyle smiled, remembering her description of the holidays. How her soft green eyes lit up when she talked about her brothers and their wives and children. She actually liked all of them and enjoyed being with them. Kyle, on the other hand, dreaded spending time in the company of his parents and brother, and the only reason he ever did was for his grandfather's sake.

He knew Rebecca considered her family to be normal, but Kyle thought the Taylors sounded almost too good to be true. In fact, if he hadn't gotten to know Rebecca so well and known how honest she was, he would have doubted any family could be like hers.

The thoughts of Rebecca's family reminded him that his grandfather wasn't the only person he would hate to leave. It would also be tough to say goodbye to Rebecca. With her he had the first long-term, close female relationship that didn't include sexual intimacy, and it was a continuing source of amazement to him how much her friendship had come to mean. It also amazed him that she was still unmarried, but selfishly, he was glad. If Rebecca were to marry, he was sure their friendship would never survive. In Kyle's experience, most men couldn't handle their wives having male friends.

Yes, he would miss her a lot.

He would especially miss their daily talks—knowing that, if he needed a sounding board, she was there. He would also miss teasing her. He chuckled, thinking about how much fun she was to tease, because she was so all-fired ladylike and proper.

He looked at his watch. He had a half hour before he had to leave for his lunch meeting with the advertising director of an HMO the agency was trying to land. He decided to see if Rebecca was in her office. He was eager to discuss the new job with her. But before he could get out the door, his phone rang. And by the time the conversation had concluded, it was time to go to lunch.

The talk with Rebecca would have to wait.

"You busy?"

Rebecca stretched. She'd been reading and editing copy for hours. "Actually, I need a break. Come on in."

JoBeth Weaver, looking smart and sophisticated in a cream wool suit worn with cream stockings and cocoa suede pumps, walked into the office and sat in the same chair Kyle had occupied earlier. Her outfit was a perfect complement to her short russet hair and nut brown eyes. She leaned back, crossing her legs and studying Rebecca. Each gesture was unhurried and elegant.

Rebecca wished, for perhaps the thousandth time, that she had even half the style and dash of JoBeth. "What's up?" she said, rolling her head in slow circles to work out the kinks in her neck.

"Have you heard about Kyle?"

"What about him?"

"Chloe told me Mark offered Kyle the chance to head up a new office in L.A. and that he's accepted."

Rebecca felt as if she'd been punched. She struggled to keep her composure. As much as she liked JoBeth, and as close as the two women had become, Rebecca had never revealed her true feelings about Kyle. She wanted no one, not even JoBeth, feeling sorry for her. "When did this happen?" she managed to say in an almost normal voice.

"This morning."

"Kyle mentioned a meeting with Mark, but I haven't talked to him since." Why hadn't Kyle told her? If the shoe were on the other foot and Rebecca had been offered a big, new job, Kyle would have been the first person she'd tell.

Yes, but you're in love with him, and he's not in love with you.

"I don't think Kyle's told anyone," JoBeth said, her brown eyes altogether too sharp for Rebecca's comfort. "And Mark would probably strangle Chloe if he knew she'd spilled the beans."

"If Mark wanted it to be a secret, he shouldn't have let her know about it," Rebecca pointed out. Mark's secretary was a notorious blabbermouth, but she was also highly efficient and extremely good-hearted, so everyone overlooked the one flaw.

"So what do you think?"

By now Rebecca had gotten her turbulent emotions under control, and she was once more her composed, quiet self. "It sounds like a wonderful opportunity for Kyle."

"Yes it does." JoBeth waited a heartbeat. "So you're happy for him?"

"Of course. Why wouldn't I be?"

JoBeth shrugged. "The two of you have been pretty tight. I just thought you might—"

"JoBeth," Rebecca said firmly, "I am thrilled for Kyle, just as I'd be thrilled for you if you had an opportunity to move up." Briskly now, she added, "So when is he leaving? We're going to have to have a big send-off party."

"I don't have any of the details. Only that he is. I would imagine, though, that it'll take some time to get everything set up."

Rebecca nodded. Her mind was spinning, but she couldn't allow herself to think about this news and what it meant until JoBeth was gone.

"Won't be the same around here without him, will it?" JoBeth said.

"No, it won't." Rebecca forced herself to toss off a lighthearted chuckle. "Who's going to proposition us behind the water cooler now?"

JoBeth made a face. "Not to worry. I'm sure Dell will be glad to take up the slack." She stood, smoothing down her skirt. "Think I'll go congratulate Kyle. Want to come?"

"No, I better not. I've got to finish this." Rebecca indicated the abandoned copy. "I'll see him later."

After JoBeth left, Rebecca got up and shut her office door. She leaned against it for a long moment, closing her eyes and telling herself not to be an idiot. But she couldn't help it. She was ridiculously close to tears. Dangerously close to tears.

Kyle was leaving.

Moving 2400 miles away.

She bit her bottom lip to still its trembling.

You knew nothing would ever come of your feelings for him. So what's the big deal? Won't it actually be easier for you if he's not around? Maybe that way you'll finally be able to forget about him. Now pull yourself together. When he does get around to telling you about this, you can't let him suspect how upset you are.

She took several deep breaths, then opened her eyes and walked back to her desk. Calling on the determination and inner strength that were the hallmarks of her personality, she swept her mind free of the turmoil JoBeth's news had produced. She even managed a wry smile.

Like Scarlett O'Hara, she would think about this, if not tomorrow, then after she'd reached the privacy of her own home.

Damn that Chloe! What a big mouth she had. After JoBeth left his office, Kyle, still cussing out the hapless Chloe, headed straight for Rebecca's.

Her door was closed.

Odd. She never closed her door. Mark's open-door policy was usually followed by all the employees.

Kyle knocked, then opened the door without waiting for an answer.

"Well, hi," Rebecca said, turning away from her computer terminal. "I hear congratulations are in order." She swiveled her chair to face him completely, unconsciously smoothing the sides of her dark blond hair, which didn't need smoothing at all, before giving him a bright smile. "That's why Mark wanted to see you this morning, isn't it?"

"Yes. I could kill Chloe. I wanted to tell you about it myself. In fact, I started to come—"

"Oh, don't be silly. It doesn't matter. This is so exciting! When are you going?"

For some reason, Kyle felt an odd sense of disappointment. Didn't she even *care* that he was moving so far away? "We're targeting May 1 as the official opening day, but I'll be back and forth long before then. I'll probably be going out for a preliminary investigation in February."

"Investigation?"

"You know. To look at office space, that kind of thing."

"Oh. Of course." She smiled again. "You'll like that. Getting away from the snow and cold."

"That's definitely one of the big pluses."

"And just think of all that new romantic territory," she said teasingly. "All those California golden girls."

He laughed on cue, vainly trying to stifle his growing sense of dissatisfaction with her reaction to his news. "Another plus."

"Well, I can't wait to hear all the details, but right now I've simply got to finish this report. I promised Dell it would be on his desk by five."

She was treating this so casually. As if it were just another business development and not important on a personal level at all. What was wrong with her? Was she jealous because he'd been offered this opportunity? Was that what was behind this uncharacteristic behavior?

For a moment, he considered bluntly asking her. After all, they'd always been honest with each other. But the words stuck in his throat, and he found himself saying instead, "That's okay. I have things to do myself." Earlier, he'd planned to ask her to have dinner with him, but now he felt awkward about that, too. "Well, I'll see you tomorrow, I guess."

"Okay." Another bright smile. "Congratulations again. You deserve this." So saying, she turned her attention back to her computer terminal.

As Kyle walked back to his office, he told himself maybe he was imagining things. Maybe she really was just busy. But always before, when he'd wanted to talk, she'd put aside everything.

Something was definitely wrong. It was not like Rebecca to act this way.

Chapter Two

Rebecca stared unseeingly out the window of the Rapid as it bore her to Shaker Heights, where she parked her car each morning.

She had acted like an idiot when Kyle came to her office. Good grief, what was wrong with her? She knew he was confused by her false cheer and stupid remarks.

Why *couldn't* she have just acted natural? It wasn't as if she hadn't had plenty of practice in disguising her real feelings.

But the news of his impending move had been such a shock. So totally unexpected. She'd had no time to prepare. No time to get that armor of hers in place.

What must he be thinking?

On and on her thoughts went as she continued to berate herself. By the time she finally reached her apartment in Chagrin Falls, after contending with slippery roads and heavy traffic on top of her inner turmoil, she was exhausted on every level.

Even the simple tasks of feeding Mariah, her twelve-year-old tortoiseshell cat and nuking a frozen dinner—which she had no appetite for, anyway—were too much to contend with.

At eight-thirty, she took two aspirin and went to bed. She fell asleep almost immediately.

The baby was the most beautiful child Rebecca had ever seen. She marveled that she had produced such perfection. She would never tire of looking at him. Her son. Hers and Kyle's. The baby had fat cheeks and a dimpled chin and his father's eyes—blue as a summer sky. There was too little hair to know what color it would be, but it didn't matter. Although Rebecca knew she wasn't beautiful, she did have great hair— thick and dark gold, and of course, Kyle's hair was wonderful. But then, everything about Kyle was wonderful, just as everything about his son was wonderful. She looked from the baby to her husband. "He's so perfect, isn't he?"

Kyle beamed at her from his chair at the side of her hospital bed. "My love, of course, he's perfect. After all, you're his mother."

Rebecca's heart swelled with happiness. "Shall we name him Graham, sweetheart?" Now the baby was searching, turning his head toward her breast and opening his mouth.

"Nothing would make me happier. Graham Donald MacNeill the Third. Grandfather will be so pleased." Kyle leaned over to kiss her as she opened her gown and guided the baby's eager mouth to her nipple. Kyle watched, a look of utter tenderness on his

face. Their gazes met above the baby's head. "Thank you, my darling," he whispered. "I love you."

"And I love you," Rebecca said. She was the luckiest woman in the world, and she knew it.

The jangle of the alarm woke her at five-thirty. Automatically she reached out to shut it off, simultaneously throwing off the covers and getting up. Shivering, still half-asleep, she headed for the bathroom.

Five minutes later, face washed, bundled into her terry-cloth robe and slippers, she shuffled into the kitchen. She yawned, coffee the only thought in her head. But just as she reached for the cord to plug in her coffeemaker, the dream came rushing back, bringing with it a barrage of emotions.

The scene in the hospital was as real to her as if it had happened yesterday. She could even feel the downy softness of the baby's skin, hear his soft grunts as he suckled at her breast and smell the combination of milk and talcum and sweet baby that clung to him.

Knowing it had only been a dream, that the likelihood of it ever happening was nonexistent, caused an emptiness and sense of loss that was so profound, it was almost a physical pain.

In that moment, she knew she'd been kidding herself. She would never forget Kyle. He was as much a part of her as her fingers or her toes.

She also knew that she would do anything, anything at all, to have his baby.

Kyle removed his topcoat, hung it in his office closet, picked up his coffee mug and headed for the kitchenette. After filling his mug and grabbing one of the glazed doughnuts out of the open box sitting on the counter, he walked toward Rebecca's office.

This morning her door was open, and she was already hard at work, even though it was only a few minutes past eight.

She looked up as he walked in. "Don't you know doughnuts are loaded with fat?" Her smile was natural and welcoming.

Kyle grinned. "What's your point?" He still had no idea what was behind her bewildering behavior yesterday afternoon, but whatever it was, it seemed to be gone this morning, he realized with relief.

"My point is that sooner or later all this junk you eat is going to take its toll."

"I don't consider doughnuts junk. Now eggplant and cabbage and zucchini and all that other stuff you like so much—that's what I call junk."

She shook her head. "I give up."

"You? You never give up. You'll be on my case again next week." He sat down and drank some of his coffee while wolfing down the remains of the doughnut.

The teasing light in her eyes faded, and she cocked her head in that way she had when she was thinking hard about something. "You know, it's funny you should say that, because only this morning, I was thinking the same thing."

"What? That you'll be on my case again next week?"

"No, that I'm not a quitter. That if I want something badly enough, I ought to be able to figure out a way to get it."

"Hey, I'd put my money on you every time."

She picked up her own coffee mug and drank from it, eyeing him over the rim.

Not for the first time, Kyle thought what beautiful eyes she had. They were her best feature: big and green and flecked with gold. She'd told him the eyes were a Taylor family trademark, that her mother and several of her brothers had them, too. This morning, they were speculative, and Kyle wondered what it was she wanted that had triggered the assessment of herself that she'd mentioned. He was just about to ask her when she spoke.

"So tell me all about the new job."

For the next twenty minutes, he repeated everything Mark had told him, and Rebecca listened, interjecting a comment occasionally. When he was finished, she said, "I'm really glad for you, Kyle."

"Thanks."

"But it won't be the same around here without you."

"Look at the bright side. No one to bug you."

She smiled.

Their eyes met.

A long moment passed.

"I'm going to miss you," he said softly. "That's the downside about this job. Leaving my grandfather. And leaving you."

She looked away, but not before he'd caught the flicker of emotion in her eyes. She felt bad, too. The knowledge warmed Kyle. Suddenly it was important to say what he was feeling. "Your friendship has meant a lot to me, you know that, don't you?"

She nodded but didn't answer.

"And I'll never forget that you saved my life."

Her eyes slowly met his again, and now he saw the sparkle of tears on her lashes.

Tenderness flooded him. His voice was gruff as he added, "I've said this before, and it won't change just because I'm leaving. If there's ever anything, anything at all, you need or want, all you have to do is ask."

Long after Kyle left her office, Rebecca kept hearing his voice as he'd said, "If there's ever anything, anything at all, you need or want, all you have to do is ask...."

I want your baby.

What if she were to say just that?

She almost laughed aloud, imagining the look of incredulity on Kyle's face. He would be astounded, not to mention horrified. Well, no wonder. It was a crazy idea.

And yet...

Was it so crazy?

Yes, it's crazy. What are you thinking of?

Over the next hour, as she tried to concentrate on her work, the idea churned. No matter how many times she told herself it was nutty, the idea refused to go away.

Okay, think about it.

If she couldn't have Kyle—and she knew she couldn't—why couldn't she at least have his baby?

Because he doesn't want kids, Rebecca. He's said so, flat out.

But what if there were some way she could have Kyle's baby without him being involved at all?

Ha! That's really funny. What is this going to be? An immaculate conception?

No, of course not. But lots of women raised their children alone. Kyle wouldn't have to be involved at all once he impregnated her.

And just how are you going to get him to do that?

Well, he *was* always propositioning her. And granted, Rebecca knew his suggestive comments were mostly made because he enjoyed teasing her, but he still made them. What if, the next time he said something about "showing her his etchings" or "making beautiful music together" she were to say, "Okay, let's do it," and not let him off the hook when he tried to back down.

It wouldn't be easy to call his bluff, but she could pull it off. She knew she could.

What about birth control? Kyle's too smart not to use a condom.

She would tell him he didn't need to use anything because she was on the Pill.

But you'd be deceiving him.

Rebecca bit her lip. He would never forgive her if she tricked him. It wasn't as if she could keep a pregnancy secret. Kyle would be bound to find out, and then he would know the baby was his. He would be angry and resentful, thinking she had done it to get him to marry her. The only way she could hide a pregnancy would be to quit her job and move away.

But then she'd never see Kyle again.

And where could she go? She would have to go back to Houston. And Kyle knew all about her family. Wouldn't he be bound to wonder why she had dropped out of sight? Wouldn't he look for her?

Think about it, Rebecca. If the situations were reversed, if Kyle up and disappeared one day, wouldn't you be concerned? Wouldn't you eventually call his grandfather and try to find out where he was, what was wrong?

Oh, God, she couldn't do it.

It would be wrong on too many levels. Not only that, she couldn't stand the thought of never seeing Kyle again. Maybe she only had a small portion of him now, but at least she had that.

She told herself to forget the whole crazy idea.

"Ready for lunch?" JoBeth said, poking her head into Rebecca's office a few minutes after twelve.

"More than ready."

Fifteen minutes later, the two of them were seated across from each other at one of the small tables in a cafe a few doors down from their office building on Superior. The restaurant was steamy with warmth and filled with the hubbub of dozens of workers on their lunch hour. Rebecca took a bite of her tuna-filled croissant and gazed around.

A few tables away, a young mother sat eating with one hand while simultaneously jiggling a baby in the other arm. Rebecca watched her the way she watched all mothers of small children—with a mixture of envy and curiosity. She marveled at the mother's dexterity even as she wondered who she was and why she had dragged her baby out on a cold day like today.

"You're awfully quiet today," JoBeth said.

Rebecca wrenched her gaze away from the other table. She met her friend's curious eyes. "JoBeth, do you ever think about having children?"

"Me? God, no. I had enough of snotty-nosed kids when I was growing up to last me my entire lifetime."

JoBeth was the oldest of five, but unlike Rebecca, who loved being part of a big family, JoBeth had hated every minute of her childhood. Of course, she'd grown up in rural Alabama, and her family was dirt-poor. On top of that, JoBeth's mother was frail and sick much of the time, and JoBeth had been expected to take up the slack. She'd once told Rebecca it had been a miracle she'd managed to graduate from high school. Rebecca, on the other hand, had been the adored sister whose brothers doted on her.

"Why?" JoBeth said. "You still feeling the urge?"

"More than ever. In fact... I've actually been considering... artificial insemination."

JoBeth's eyes widened. "You're kidding."

"No, I'm not."

"But why such drastic measures? Why don't you just adopt a kid?"

Rebecca shrugged. "I don't know. I've thought about adoption. But there are several problems with that scenario. First of all, it's hard for a single woman to adopt a baby. Second, and I know this is probably terribly selfish, but I can't help how I feel. I want to experience giving birth."

JoBeth grimaced. "Well, to each his own."

"You think I'm crazy, don't you?"

"It doesn't matter what I think. It's your life. My philosophy is, if that's what you want, go for it."

If there's ever anything you want, all you have to do is ask.

Go for it.

If there's ever anything you want, all you have to do is ask.

Go for it.

"What do you think, Rebecca?"

Rebecca jumped. Eight pairs of eyes were watching her. She could feel her face heating. Oh my God, she'd been daydreaming through the meeting, and now, obviously, someone had asked her a question and she had no idea who or what had been said. "I'm sorry. I, uh, what did you say?" She addressed the question to Mark.

"I wondered what you thought about Dell's idea for the Howard Care Centers campaign," Mark said, his eyes twinkling.

Thank goodness, Mark was such a nice guy. Another person might have enjoyed embarrassing her by making a snide remark. "I think it has merit," she said. "However, there are some elements that bother me." She launched into her reasons for feeling the suggested television spots might be too heavy-handed in their obvious scare tactics.

After the meeting concluded, Kyle walked over to her and waited while she gathered up her papers. "Do you want go down to The Flats for dinner after work?"

"Oh, I'm sorry, I can't. Tonight's chorale practice."

"That's right. I forgot. Every Wednesday."

"Yes."

"Guess I'll have to find some other beautiful woman to keep me company." He affected a hangdog face.

Rebecca gave him a quizzical look. "What about Suzanne?" Suzanne Coltrane, a local TV personality, was Kyle's latest squeeze.

Kyle shrugged. "We called it quits. She decided she's interested in getting married, after all." His voice dripped with disgust. "Why is it women say one thing but mean another?"

"Not all women," Rebecca reminded him.

"No." He smiled. "You're the exception. You're the most honest person I know—next to me, of course. Sure you won't pass on chorale practice and keep me company?"

"No, I can't. And don't expect me to feel sorry for you, either. You'll line up another dinner companion within five minutes of picking up the phone."

"But she won't be you."

"That's because there's only one me." Rebecca was amazed that she could so easily talk the talk he expected. She was also grateful. Above all, she did not want Kyle to know how she felt. Or what she was thinking.

"That's what I like. A woman who knows her own worth."

"You like anything in skirts."

He grinned. "See what a nice guy I am? I don't take offense, even when you're insulting me."

"It's not an insult to state the truth," Rebecca pointed out. But she grinned, too.

"If you can't have dinner with me tonight, how about Friday? We'll go to Angelo's," he said, naming their favorite Italian restaurant.

"You've got a date."

Kyle decided to skip dinner out and go to see his grandfather instead. So when he got back to his office, he called his grandfather's house. "You feeling well enough for company tonight?"

"I'm always feeling well enough to see you," his grandfather said. "Plan to stay for dinner."

It was a few minutes before six-thirty when Kyle arrived at the Fairmount Boulevard mansion on Cleveland's near east side. His grandfather had purchased the redbrick Georgian home forty-seven years ago and, if anything, the house and surrounding grounds had only become more beautiful over the years. Hugo, his grandfather's companion and faithful servant for more than two decades, opened the door and gave Kyle a welcoming smile.

"Mr. MacNeill is in the study," Hugo said, taking Kyle's coat. "I'll bring you a drink. Your grandfather is having Scotch."

"What else?" Kyle said.

Graham MacNeill's study was Kyle's favorite room in the entire twenty-three-room house. It was large—about sixteen by twenty feet—and paneled in warm, golden-toned walnut. It faced south, and had a huge fireplace, so the room was always warm, even on the coldest winter nights.

Tonight, the book-lined walls and rich, jewel-toned carpet glowed from the firelight, and the smell of cedar permeated the air.

Kyle's grandfather, still a good-looking man at eighty-six, with a full head of white hair and the same blue eyes as his grandson, sat in one of the two deep-cushioned leather chairs that flanked the fireplace. He was dressed in gray slacks, a matching gray cashmere sweater and a dark green tweed jacket. His feet rested on an ottoman, and Princess, his golden retriever, lay on the floor at his side. He smiled as Kyle entered the room. Princess's tail wagged, but she didn't move from her post.

After greeting the older man and inquiring after his health, petting the dog's head and being given a drink by Hugo, Kyle sat down across from his grandfather and said, "You look much better."

"I feel much better."

After a moment, Kyle said, "I've got some news."

Graham smiled. "I thought there might be a special reason why you were coming tonight."

Kyle watched his grandfather's face for any signs of distress as he told him about the job offer.

"You've accepted, I take it?" Graham said when Kyle was finished.

"Yes."

Graham slowly sipped at his drink. "Well, I can't pretend I won't miss having you here in Cleveland, my boy, but I realize this is a good opportunity for you."

"And I'll visit often," Kyle said. "Fly in for a weekend every couple of months."

His grandfather smiled. "And I may surprise you and come out there to visit. Give those starlets in Hollywood a thrill."

Kyle laughed and heaved an inward sigh of relief. His grandfather wasn't upset. Now he could go to California with a clear mind and know that the people he cared about here were going to be fine without him.

Okay, so she couldn't trick Kyle into getting her pregnant. But what if she *did* come right out and ask him? Hadn't he said he would give her anything?

...All you have to do is ask.

What if she presented it to him as a strictly business proposition? They could even draw up a legal contract. She would stipulate that he would have no responsibility toward her or her child—either financial or moral.

His only role would be to impregnate her.

And afterward, when she had the baby, she would be on her own. The child would be hers to raise. She would neither expect nor demand anything further of him.

It could work!

And the reason it could work was because Kyle wouldn't be around. He'd be in L.A., completely removed from contact with her or any reminders of his part in her becoming a mother.

Excitement built as the idea grabbed hold. Yes, yes, this was doable. It definitely could work.

But should she do it? This was a very serious, life-changing step she was thinking of making. She needed to consider all of the ramifications.

Like, was it really right or fair of her to consider bringing a child into the world knowing that child would never have a father? Weren't there enough fatherless children out there? Was this idea of Rebecca's irresponsible?

No. She didn't think it was irresponsible to want a child and plan to raise it on her own. After all, she was a grown woman, not a teenager. She was educated. She had a good income. And she had a lot of family support. She could give a child a full, good life.

That night she could hardly sleep.

Kyle's baby.

A part of Kyle that would belong to her forever.

And all she had to do was ask.

Chapter Three

"**I**s something bothering you?" JoBeth asked. "You've been awfully quiet for the past couple of days."

"No, everything's fine," Rebecca said quickly. It was Friday morning, and for the past two days she had been entirely preoccupied with thoughts of her plan. And although she'd taken pains to act normal, obviously JoBeth had picked up some vibes. "I've just been thinking about, you know...what we talked about at lunch the other day."

JoBeth frowned. "Having a baby, you mean?"

"Will you *please* lower your voice?" Rebecca pointed to JoBeth's open door. "I really don't care to become fodder for office gossip."

"Sorry." JoBeth picked at a piece of nonexistent lint on her tangerine wool skirt. When she looked up, her brown eyes were thoughtful. "I was afraid you might be upset about Kyle leaving."

"Me? Why would I be upset? I told you, this is a marvelous opportunity for him. I'm *thrilled* for him." *Easy, easy, don't overdo it....*

JoBeth gave a little shrug and didn't press the issue. Thank goodness, Rebecca thought, and resolved to be more careful.

All of her thinking had brought about a decision. She was going to broach the subject of a baby when she was out with Kyle tonight. Not at the restaurant. She didn't want to do it in public. Instead, she would ask him to come to her place afterward. If necessary, she would say there was something she wanted to discuss in private.

Throughout the day, her stomach was filled with butterflies. Yet, no matter how nervous she felt, her resolve strengthened as the hours went by.

The bottom line was she wanted Kyle's baby. And this was her one and only chance to accomplish that goal.

So no matter how hard it would be to introduce the subject and stand her ground if Kyle was less than enthusiastic, she would do it.

Nothing worth having comes easily, Rebecca's mother was fond of saying. And Rebecca couldn't imagine anything more worth having than Kyle's baby.

The only question was, would Kyle say yes?

Kyle whistled as he strode down the hall. He was looking forward to the evening. He liked going to Angelo's and he liked going in Rebecca's company.

Once again, he realized how much he would miss her when he moved to California. When he was with her, he had the best of both worlds: the company of an attractive, intelligent woman but without the stress and demands of a romantic entanglement.

He wondered if she would ever marry. Once, he'd asked her about it, and she'd said she was picky, and so far no one had measured up to her standards. Kyle knew she'd dated several men during the past two years, but nothing ever seemed to come of it.

By now, he'd reached Rebecca's office, but she wasn't there. He sat down to wait, noticing how neat her desktop was, how neat the entire office was. As he looked around, his gaze landed on her framed citation—the one she'd gotten for saving his life. Every time he saw it, he realized anew how much he owed her.

Of course, he never wanted anything bad to happen to her, but if she ever needed anything, he hoped she would come to him. He owed her big time, and he'd love the chance to repay her.

"You haven't been waiting long, have you?"

He turned at the sound of her voice. "Nope. Just got here."

She was rubbing some kind of lotion into her hands. She smiled. "I'm almost ready."

"Take your time."

She finished with the lotion and walked over to the coat tree in the corner. He got up and took her coat from her. The light fragrance she wore was very nice, he thought, as he held her coat for her. He hated the heavy, musky perfumes so many women seemed to favor.

Rebecca's subtle scent was typical of her. Everything she wore, everything she did was low-key—pleasing and ladylike.

She was the kind of woman who fit in anywhere. Men liked her because she was smart and had a sense of humor and she was comfortable to be around. Women liked her because they trusted her.

Kyle would have liked her even if she'd had two heads, he thought in some amusement. Anyone who saves your life is bound to be right up there on your preferred people list.

They listened to a Mozart concerto as they drove to the restaurant, which was in University Heights. Kyle took his time. They were in no hurry.

Angelo, a big, dark-haired, dark-eyed man in his late forties, who had once jokingly told Kyle he wanted to be buried with a plate of lasagna in his casket, greeted them personally, as he did all his customers. "Hey, Kyle, Rebecca, good to see you. How's it goin'?"

"Going great," they answered in unison.

"How's Marge?" Rebecca said, referring to Angelo's wife, who sometimes helped out when her husband was short of wait staff.

"Ah, she's the same as ever. Still putting up with me," he joked.

The restaurant was crowded, but Angelo found them a table in the corner, and soon they were seated with glasses of red wine and a basket of hot garlic bread in front of them.

Kyle looked around to see what new memorabilia Angelo had hung on the walls. He always got a kick out of the decor, which mainly consisted of posters depicting various players on the Cleveland Indians baseball team and framed photographs of the Cleveland skyline. Angelo boasted that he was the Cleveland Indians' greatest fan. Basketball was more Kyle's game, but even he had gotten caught up in World Series fever the past couple of years.

"So what's it going to be today?" asked their waitress, a perky college student from nearby John Carroll.

Rebecca ordered the baked ziti with eggplant and Kyle ordered the lasagna with sausage.

"What did your grandfather have to say about you moving?" she asked once the waitress had left.

"He took it well. I was relieved, too. I don't know what I would've done if he had been upset. I'm not sure I could have gone." Kyle reached for a bread stick.

"I figured he'd understand. After all, he was young once, too... and ambitious." She drank some of her wine. "How'd the meeting with Gambrell go today?"

"Better than I expected." Kyle went on to describe the points they'd covered.

For the next half hour, as they ate their salads, and drank their wine, they continued to discuss work. When their main course came, they ate without talking for a while. Then Rebecca said, "Are you still working with the night basketball league?"

"Yes. Why?"

"You haven't mentioned it in a while, and I just wondered."

"I go every Thursday night." Kyle had been one of a group of men who worked out at a downtown health club and who had organized the league with the idea that it would help keep inner-city youth off the streets at night by giving them a place to go where they'd be safe from danger. One of the men had read about another city with a program like it, and he'd suggested it to the others. The program was now sponsored by a local church, and the men took regular turns coaching and playing with the youngsters.

"You like working with those kids, don't you?"

"Yes. It's satisfying to see what a difference the program has made in their lives. Now they have a place to go where they can do something they enjoy... and no one hassles them." Kyle would miss the kids, especially a boy named Enos whom he'd gotten especially close to.

Rebecca smiled and turned her attention back to her meal. For a while they ate quietly and companionably. That was another thing Kyle enjoyed about Rebecca's company. Silence didn't bother her. So many women seemed to be incapable of letting two seconds go by without filling it with noise.

After their plates had been cleared, Rebecca said, "Why don't you come out to my place for dessert? I baked a lemon meringue pie last night."

"How can I say no to that?" Lemon meringue pie was Kyle's favorite, and Rebecca knew it.

It was only eight-fifteen when they left, but the temperature had dropped and the wind had picked up.

Stars glittered overhead, snow crunched underfoot and their breath puffed out in front of them as they walked to Kyle's BMW. The drive to Van Aken Boulevard where Rebecca caught the Rapid every morning only took a few minutes. She pointed out her little Mazda, and Kyle pulled up next to it.

"See you there," she said.

All the way home Rebecca rehearsed what she would say. She was so nervous, she was practically jumping out of her skin. What would Kyle's response be when she asked him? *Please, God, don't let him say no. I want this so badly.*

As she had dozens of times in the past couple of days, she tried to think of every possible objection he might raise. She had logical answers for all of them.

Still, what if she'd forgotten something really important?

You didn't forget anything. Now settle down.

Thirty-five minutes after they'd left the restaurant she pulled into the driveway of the Chagrin Falls duplex where she had lived ever since moving to the Cleveland area. Seconds later, Kyle pulled in behind her.

Rebecca shivered as she walked toward him. She lived on a hill and there wasn't a lot of protection from the wind. She liked the location, though, because it was within walking distance of downtown and the Falls, so she hadn't considered moving. Besides, the rent was right, her landlady was wonderful and her neighbors were all really nice. And, now, with the possibility that she might have a baby, there would be all the more reason to stay here where she felt secure and comfortable.

All these thoughts tumbled through her mind as Kyle followed her inside. They entered through the enclosed back porch, and divested themselves of their boots before going into the apartment. Once inside, Rebecca headed for the living room, switching on lights as she went. Mariah, who had been sleeping on the couch, hopped off as Rebecca and Kyle entered the room. Tail up, she gave Kyle a wide berth on her way to greet Rebecca.

"Still doesn't like me, huh?" Kyle said.

Rebecca chuckled. "Cats are very set in their ways, especially this cat. Maybe after she's known you longer, she'll warm up to you."

"When, in about twenty years?" Kyle joked. He removed his coat.

"Here, let me take that. Make yourself comfortable. I'll be right back."

He heard her opening the hall closet, then bustling around in the kitchen.

"I'm making coffee. That okay?" she called.

"Yeah, sure." Kyle looked around. He liked her living room. It was homey, he thought. Comfortable. Like Rebecca. The colors were warm: reds and browns and yellows. And there were plants and needlepoint pillows and books everywhere.

Kyle settled into the deep-cushioned couch and loosened his tie. That was the only bad thing about going somewhere straight after work. He couldn't change clothes. He rested his head back against the cushions and closed his eyes. He hadn't gotten much sleep the past few days. Man, he was tired....

"Kyle?"

Kyle opened his eyes.

Rebecca stood there, smiling down at him. She'd changed from her gray suit and light green blouse into well-worn jeans and a red turtleneck sweater. Red socks covered her feet. She'd even taken her hair down, and it fell in loose, shining waves around her face, making her look softer and younger. "You fell asleep," she said.

Kyle shook his head to clear it. "I guess I did. Sorry."

"I don't mind. There's your coffee and pie." She motioned toward the coffee table. "I'll just go get mine."

A few minutes later, she was back. Kyle finished off his pie within minutes, then leaned back and drank his coffee slowly. It tasted good.

"Kyle..."

He turned to look at Rebecca, who sat on the other end of the couch. She had curled her feet up under her and was leaning forward slightly. Her eyes, always so quiet and thoughtful, seemed very bright. He smiled curiously. "What?"

She didn't answer for a long moment. Long enough so that Kyle felt a trickle of apprehension.

"You know how you've said if I ever wanted anything—"

"All you have to do is ask," he finished for her.

"Well, there *is* something."

The expression in her eyes increased his feeling of disquiet. What was wrong? Was she in some kind of trouble? "Name it. It's yours."

"First I have to explain. This... this is something I want desperately." Her voice trembled slightly. "I have wanted it desperately for a long time, but I had just about despaired of ever getting it."

Kyle was totally bewildered. What was it that had her so rattled? He couldn't imagine.

"But now," she said slowly, "you can give it to me."

"I told you. Just name it."

She met his gaze unflinchingly. "I want you to give me a baby."

"What?" Kyle couldn't believe he'd heard her correctly. "You're kidding, right?"

"I've never been more serious."

Kyle's mind spun. Holy smoke! She certainly sounded serious.

"Look, I've thought it all out." Now her voice was eager, excited. "I know you don't want children. Well, you wouldn't have any responsibility here at all. The child would be mine and mine alone. Your total contribution would be to get me pregnant."

"Rebecca..." Surely she wasn't serious. She *couldn't* be serious.

"Just hear me out, okay?"

He sighed. "Okay."

"I've thought this through very carefully. I think we should draw up a formal agreement stating that I will assume complete financial and moral responsibility for any child we have. You would be completely free."

"But, Rebecca—"

"Please, Kyle, don't say no. Listen to me. Think about this. I want a child so badly. I'm not getting any younger, and my childbearing years are disappearing fast. I know, you're probably thinking why you? And the answer is that I want the father of my child to be someone I admire and respect. I can't think of anyone I admire and respect more than I do you."

Rebecca could see that he was completely dumbfounded by her proposition, so much so that he was having trouble speaking. *Please, God,* she prayed, *let him agree.*

He stared at her. "I'm flattered that you feel that way, I really am. I mean, who wouldn't be. But I can't do it. Ask me something else, anything else, but not this."

Rebecca's heart sank. Oh, God, he wasn't going to agree. "This is the only thing I want. Having a child of my own means more to me than anything in the world." She took a deep breath and prepared to play her final card. "You said all I had to do was name it and it would be mine."

He ran his hands through his hair. "I'm sorry," he said. "I wish I could do this for you, but I can't. I know what I said, but I never dreamed you'd want something like this."

Rebecca's gaze never wavered. "I guess I misunderstood. I guess I didn't realize there were conditions on your promise. I guess I thought when you said *anything, anything at all,* you meant just that."

"Rebecca, be reasonable. You know how I feel about marriage and children."

"I'm not asking you to marry me. I'm just asking you to impregnate me." What could she say to persuade him? She *had* to persuade him, dammit! She would not let him renege on his promise.

"But—"

"Haven't you been trying to get me in the sack for the past two years?" she pressed on implacably. "Well, now's your chance. Gee, Kyle, I would think you'd leap at this opportunity. Unless, of course, you didn't mean *that,* either. Just like you never meant your promise." She knew she was dangerously close to tears. She swallowed hard. She didn't want to cry in front of him. It was bad enough that she was practically begging.

Kyle's eyes darkened. "That's a cheap shot."

He wasn't going to do it. She had gambled, and she had lost. Trying to still the trembling inside her, she took refuge in anger. "Fine. I'm sorry I put you on the spot." She stood. "I'm really tired. I'll get your coat." She walked out into the hall.

He followed her. "Dammit, Rebecca, you're not being fair! If it was anything else . . ."

"I don't want anything else." She opened the closet, removed his topcoat and handed it to him. "Forget about it. I'm sorry I asked."

He reached for her hand, but she moved back.

"Come on, Rebecca. You're being completely unreasonable."

"Good night, Kyle." She no longer wanted to discuss the subject. She just wanted him to leave.

"I'm sorry," he said again.

She shrugged, the effort costing her more in will-power than she'd known she had. "Don't lose any sleep over it," she said. "Thanks for dinner. It was lovely, as always."

He rubbed his forehead, looked as if he were going to say something else, then expelled a noisy breath, gave her another I-can't-believe-this-is-happening look, put his topcoat on, and left.

Five minutes later, she heard the sound of his car starting.

It was only then that she burst into tears.

Many hours later, as Kyle lay awake in his river-front condominium, he thought about the hurt look in Rebecca's eyes. He kept replaying their conversation over and over in his mind, wondering if he could have done anything or said anything differently.

He'd not only hurt her, he'd let her down. After all his promises to the contrary, he had refused her the one thing she'd ever asked of him.

How had this happened?

He guessed he'd always known Rebecca wanted kids. Hell, she'd even mentioned her desire a couple of times, although not lately. He'd never really paid that much attention when she'd talked about kids, though, because the subject didn't interest him.

He punched up his pillow and turned on his side so he could see out the window. Clouds had moved in off the lake, and the moon was hidden behind one of them. He watched as the cloud made its slow way, exposing the milky sliver of moon bit by bit.

He remembered once, about a year ago, when he and Rebecca were working with an infant model. Throughout the shoot, Rebecca had been wonderful with the baby. But afterward, when the mother had taken the child away, a wistful look lingered in Rebecca's eyes, and she had grown very quiet.

Damn, but he felt like a jerk.

Rebecca was his best friend. A totally unselfish friend. She had risked her own life to save his. He owed her a tremendous debt, a debt that could never be repaid.

And what had he done?

The first and only time she asked him for something, something she wanted desperately, he had refused. But how could he have done anything else?

You owe her your life.

Yes, but...

All she's asking for is a life in return. That's fair, isn't it?

He fell asleep with the question still unanswered.

Rebecca usually slept late on Saturdays. It was the one day of the week when she didn't have to be anywhere at any certain time, so she took advantage of it.

The telephone woke her at eight.

"Rebecca, can I come over? I want to talk to you."

Her heart somersaulted. It was Kyle. "S-sure. I'll put the coffee on."

She waited on pins and needles. She was afraid to hope, but she couldn't help it. *Oh, God, please, please, please...*

By the time he arrived, an hour later, with a box of doughnuts in his hands, she was a wreck.

"Look," he said without preamble, "I've been thinking it over. I still think it's crazy... but because I care about you and because I owe you more than I can ever repay, I've decided to do what you want me to do."

Rebecca put her hand over her mouth. Her eyes filled with tears. "Oh, Kyle, thank you."

He held up his hand. "Wait. Before you start thanking me, let's talk about some things you don't seem to have thought of."

"Believe me, I've thought of everything."

"I'm not so sure. Here's what concerns me. Do you have any idea how rough this is going to be on you? I'll escape the worst of it, because I'll be gone. Besides, I'm a man, and whether we like to admit it or not, there's still a double standard when it comes to something like this. And you're the one who will bear the brunt of everything, because people are going to talk. Can you live with that?"

"I thought of all that and, well... I feel it would be best for everyone concerned if no one but you and me know the truth."

"How is that possible? People will see that you're pregnant."

"I know, but I thought I would tell everyone I've been artificially inseminated." Rebecca gave him a sheepish smile. "I've already laid the groundwork. I, uh, told JoBeth I was thinking about insemination."

His eyes widened. "Is *that* what you want? To be inseminated with my, uh, sperm? I thought—"

"Oh, no!" she interrupted, embarrassment causing her face to heat. She licked her lips. "Insemination is very expensive. No, I, uh, thought we'd just try the conventional method."

"So you'd just *say* you'd been inseminated."

"Yes."

Kyle nodded thoughtfully. "That could work."

"Oh, Kyle, it *will* work! I know it will." Rebecca couldn't believe this was really happening, that he'd really consented. And she was immensely relieved that he'd agreed to the insemination story. She would never have wanted anyone to know about him. That's all she'd need, for their co-workers and mutual friends to be looking at her and speculating and feeling sorry for her.

"The other thing is, I would insist on financial responsibility."

"I can't take your money!"

"Well, I can't father a child and not pay its way in the world."

"But, Kyle—"

"Unless you agree, I won't do it. We can set up some kind of trust fund if you don't want to take money directly from me. That's my condition."

Stalemate. Rebecca studied the hard edge to his chin, the stubborn glint in his blue eyes, and knew he wasn't bluffing. Well, a lot could happen between now and the birth of a baby. This battle didn't have to be fought now. "Fine."

"Good."

Silence pulsed between them. "Is—is there anything else?" she asked.

"Only, um . . . when did you want to start trying?" He didn't quite meet her eyes.

If Rebecca hadn't been so thrilled and happy, she might have laughed. Kyle was uncomfortable. This was a first. He was always so sure of himself, so at ease under all circumstances.

In some ways, his discomfort made her feel more in control, although the situation *was* awkward, and it was hard to treat it in the businesslike way she had decided upon. She must try, though.

"Late next week would be a good time," she said.

"Okay. Uh, why late next week?"

"Well, I've been taking my temperature for the past few months so that I'd know when I was ovulating and likely to get pregnant." She said this briskly, pretending this behavior wasn't the least unusual.

"I don't understand . . ."

Rebecca refused to be embarrassed. "I told you how much I want a baby. Well, I believe in being prepared. And that means knowing the optimum time of the month for me to conceive."

Amusement sparked in his eyes. "I've got to hand it to you. You think of everything."

"When it's important, yes."

"Rebecca . . ." The amusement was gone, replaced now with concern. "This *is* important. Are you sure you've really thought about it? It won't be easy for you."

"I've thought about it. I want this, Kyle. I'm willing to make any sacrifice to have it."

He nodded reluctantly. "Okay."

Rebecca smiled. It pleased her that he was worried about her, but his worrying was needless. It really was going to be okay. In fact, from now on, life would be better than okay.

It would be wonderful.

Chapter Four

After Kyle left, Rebecca walked around in a daze. She alternated between giddy happiness and excitement and horrible feelings of inadequacy and fear.

Because, no matter how many times she'd told herself she would handle the business of getting pregnant as just that—a-cut-and-dried business arrangement—the fact remained that in order for Rebecca to become pregnant with Kyle's child, the two of them would have to make love.

As in, have sex.

As in, get naked and have sex.

Rebecca sat on a kitchen chair and stared at nothing. Her heart beat harder.

She and Kyle were going to make love.

In eight days.

A week from tomorrow.

Oh my God....

Next Sunday afternoon, he was going to come to her apartment for the purpose of getting the deed done. That's what they had decided.

Dear heaven...

All sorts of previously unthought of fears battered her. What if she were a terrible disappointment to him? What if...*oh, God*...she didn't excite him?

Her face flushed as she realized they would be making love in the afternoon.

In broad daylight!

As the knowledge sank in, she wondered if she had lost her mind.

Why hadn't she insisted they do it at night? At least at night she could have had the lights off, and she wouldn't have to see any feelings of disappointment Kyle might be having.

After all, she was not exactly a sexpot, and Kyle had dated some really gorgeous, sexy women over the years. Rebecca had even met a few of them, because he'd brought them to office parties. She thought about how, without exception, his companions had had tall slender bodies and long, beautiful legs and perfect complexions and faces that would be any photographer's dream.

She closed her eyes.

She, on the other hand, was of ordinary height, with ordinary weight, and ordinary legs and a completely ordinary face. In fact, the only two attributes she possessed that were a little better than ordinary were her hair and her eyes.

How could she not have thought of all this when she'd come up with her brilliant idea? Actually, she knew why. She had been so focused on achieving the goal of getting Kyle to agree to her plan, she had not stopped to think about what would be involved if he *did* agree.

By the time she went to bed, she had worked herself into a terrible crisis of self-confidence. Maybe she *was* crazy!

And maybe tomorrow she should call Kyle and tell him to forget the entire, ill-advised idea.

By Monday Rebecca knew she was going to do no such thing. She was going through with her plan. She had calmed down greatly since her panic attack after Kyle had left her apartment on Saturday morning.

She'd concluded since she had no control over how Kyle felt, there was no percentage in worrying about it. And if he was disappointed in her, he would be too much of a gentleman to let her know it, anyway. In the end, what she didn't know couldn't hurt her. Besides, the important thing was, she would get what she wanted—a child of her own by the man she loved—and if she had to suffer through a little embarrassment to reach that goal, so be it.

Remember the end result, she told herself again and again.

You'll have Kyle's baby.

She *was* a bit worried about how Kyle would act on Monday. She hoped they could carry on the way they normally did. She didn't want anyone at the office to notice anything out of the ordinary.

But that concern was eliminated when, on reaching the office early Monday morning, she discovered Kyle would not be in all week. He had left her an e-mail saying that he would be in Los Angeles through Wednesday, then head for Houston where he would meet with Simon Christopher. "I'll see you Sunday afternoon, as planned," the message concluded.

Rebecca could actually feel her muscles relaxing. A reprieve. God was good.

For the rest of the week, she tried not to think about the upcoming weekend. For the most part, she was successful. She did decide to drop another hint Jo-Beth's way, so that when—she refused to think in terms of "if"—she became pregnant, JoBeth, at least, would be prepared for it.

With that end in mind, on Friday she invited Jo-Beth to have a drink with her after work.

"I've decided to do it," she said once they were settled in a booth at their favorite downtown pub.

"Do what?" JoBeth took a swallow of her margarita.

"Be artificially inseminated."

JoBeth fished a piece of lime out of her drink and sucked at it. Her eyes studied Rebecca.

"Well," Rebecca said, "say something."

"I can't think of anything to say."

Rebecca sighed. "Do you think people will be shocked when they find out?"

JoBeth shrugged. "Some of them. But mostly, I think, people will think you're pretty gutsy."

"Actually, I don't care what anyone else thinks." Rebecca took a sip of her sparkling Burgundy.

JoBeth grinned. "Then why'd you ask?"

After a moment, Rebecca laughed. "I don't think I realized until just this moment that I *don't* care."

"Good. If you're going to do something, and you think it's right, you should never worry about what other people think."

They smiled at each other.

"You're a good friend, you know that?" Rebecca said.

"I try."

They sat companionably silent for a while, then JoBeth said, "What about your family? Have you told them what you're planning?"

Rebecca shook her head. She'd been trying to figure out whether she should say something before the fact or not. "I don't think I'm going to tell them until it's a done deal."

"You afraid they'll try to talk you out of it?"

"Not exactly." She met JoBeth's gaze. "Well, maybe a little.... You know how it is with families. Mothers, especially."

JoBeth nodded.

"Once I'm pregnant, they'll accept it."

JoBeth nodded again. Then she smiled and raised her glass. "Well, kiddo, here's to you. I wish you luck."

Kyle tried not to think of the promise he'd made to Rebecca, but at odd times during the week, their agreement would pop into his head. He hoped he hadn't made a mistake. He knew Rebecca believed she'd considered everything when she'd asked him to give her a child, but he wasn't sure she was prepared for the actuality of it.

Kyle had many married friends, including his college roommate, whose wife had given birth to their first child the previous summer. Kyle would never forget the weekend he'd spent with Blake and Courtney in Boston when their son was about six weeks old. The baby had colic, and either one or the other of them was constantly walking with him, because otherwise he cried nonstop. Kyle had felt sorry for the poor little kid, sorrier for Courtney and even sorrier for Blake, who seemed dazed. The experience had only reinforced Kyle's ideas about marriage and kids and the whole domestic bit.

Blake had admitted to Kyle that he'd never dreamed being a father would entail so much work. "I had no idea, Kyle," he'd said when Courtney had gone out briefly to buy groceries. "Having a kid, it takes one hundred percent of your time and energy. And there are two of us. I don't know how single parents do it."

Kyle was afraid Rebecca was romanticizing parenthood. Sure, she'd been around the children of her siblings, but she hadn't lived with them, she hadn't had the twenty-four-hour-a-day care of them. She'd seen them for a few hours or a few days, when they were surrounded by a doting family who entertained them and helped take care of them. It was a whole other world when you were the only person to do all the things that needed doing.

Kyle wondered if he should try to talk to her again. Even as he wondered, he knew it would do no good.

She was determined, and when Rebecca was determined, no one could sway her from her chosen course.

She would probably view Kyle's attempt to dissuade her, or at least to make her be more realistic, as a way of weaseling his way out of something he didn't want to do.

No, there was no way out of this.

He'd promised, so he would see it through.

He only hoped Rebecca wasn't sorry later.

Sunday morning, Rebecca went to church as usual. She knew it would be best to fill up the hours before Kyle was due to arrive. Otherwise, she would just get more and more nervous.

She got home from church at twelve-thirty. He was coming at three.

She had cleaned the apartment the day before. It was spotless. This morning, before leaving for church, she'd put clean sheets on the bed and turned down the covers invitingly. She'd even closed the miniblinds so that the light in the room was muted. She decided she would close the blinds in the living room, too, just in case.

She hadn't been sure what to wear, but after much thought, she had chosen soft wool burgundy slacks and a coordinating sweater that her mother had given her for Christmas. They were comfortable and pretty, and the color flattered her. She debated on whether to wear her hair up or down, and decided on down. Her normal chignon was worn to make her appear more professional and businesslike. Down was definitely softer and, hopefully, more inviting.

She debated over jewelry and settled on her small diamond stud earrings and her watch and nothing else.

She took great care with her makeup, using more blush and eye shadow than she usually wore. Maybe she wasn't beautiful, but she certainly could try....

Finally finished dressing, she walked around the apartment and gave it a last inspection. Everything looked perfect; she couldn't think of another thing to do. For a moment, she considered putting on some soft music and maybe chilling a bottle of wine. But those ideas were quickly discarded.

She didn't want to give Kyle the idea she expected romance. She had presented her plan to him as a business proposition, so she'd better stick to that.

She looked at the clock. Were those hands even moving? She took several deep breaths. She felt half-sick.

At two-thirty the phone rang.

"Rebecca, it's Kyle."

Oh, no! He'd changed his mind!

"Listen," he said, "I've got a problem. My car won't start. I think I've got a dead battery."

Her reaction was a mixture of relief and dismay. "Oh, dear, well—"

"It's okay. I'm borrowing Jack's car. But I'll be later than we planned. Just wanted you to know."

"Don't worry about it. I'll see you when you get here." Great. Now she'd have even longer to chew her nails and be nervous.

Kyle's knock at the door finally came at three-thirty.

Rebecca pressed her fingers against her stomach, trying to still the butterflies. Her heart sped up, even as she told herself to stay calm.

She smoothed her hair, inhaled deeply, pasted a bright smile on her face and opened the door.

"Hi," he said. "I made it."

His smile wasn't quite as self-assured as it usually was. Knowing that he was uncomfortable, too, helped steady Rebecca's nerves, and her voice sounded almost normal. "Hi. Come on in."

Bringing the smell of winter and his spicy aftershave in with him, he shrugged out of his fur-lined leather jacket and handed it to her. Underneath, he wore snug-fitting jeans and a royal blue cashmere sweater that intensified the blue of his eyes. "I parked in the driveway. Is that okay? Or should I move it out to the street?"

"Does Mrs. Andrews have room to get out if she needs to?" Mrs. Andrews was Rebecca's landlady and occupied the other half of the duplex.

"Yes. I parked behind your side of the garage."

"Then it's okay. Why don't you go on into the living room? Can I get you something to drink? A beer?"

"Sure. Sounds good."

Their eyes met briefly, then each looked away. You could feel the tension in the air.

Rebecca used the time it took her to hang up his jacket and go out to the kitchen to take several deep breaths and give herself an inward pep talk. She took a cold bottle of beer out of the refrigerator, added a diet drink for herself and picked up the bowl of cashews she'd fixed earlier. Maybe the act of eating the nuts and drinking their drinks would help them relax and gradually lead up to the objective of the afternoon. *That's it. Focus on the objective and not the path necessary to get there.*

"Thanks," he said when she handed him the beer. He took a quick, long swallow.

For a second, Rebecca forgot her own anxiety. It was perverse of her, she knew, but it was kind of satisfying to see Kyle ill at ease. Again, his discomfort helped her to feel calmer.

"So Jack didn't mind you using his car?" she said. Jack Everett was Kyle's next-door neighbor and best friend ever since their high school days.

"No, he said he and Ellie were planning to stay in and watch the Ohio State game this afternoon. And they had her car if they wanted to go somewhere later." He said all this without ever meeting her eyes directly.

Rebecca nodded and couldn't think of anything else to say. It was the first time in their entire relationship that she could remember being at a loss for a topic of conversation. "They're predicting snow tonight," she finally said when the silence became oppressive.

"Yes, I know."

Silence fell between them again. Rebecca drank her drink and searched frantically for something else to say. After a few minutes, she laughed uncomfortably. "This is terribly awkward, isn't it?"

Now he looked at her. Really looked at her. And then he smiled and patted the seat beside him. "Come sit over here," he said softly.

Heart beating too fast, she put her drink down and moved to sit next to him on the couch.

He put his arm around her. With his other hand, he gently turned her face to his. "Why don't we start with a kiss?"

Rebecca couldn't have spoken if her life had depended on it. Her heart was beating too hard and too fast and too loudly. Surely he could hear it.

He lowered his head slowly.

Rebecca lifted her chin.

And they bumped noses.

"Sorry," he said.

"Oh, I'm sorry," she said.

"Shall we try again?" His eyes were filled with amusement.

Rebecca laughed in embarrassment. "I promise not to crack your nose again."

She didn't. This time she cracked his forehead. But the crack broke the remaining ice. Kyle chuckled, and Rebecca joined him. "Believe it or not, I really have done this before," he said, still laughing. "I know I can get it right."

He got it very right.

It was so right that Rebecca wanted the kiss to go on forever. His mouth slanted over hers, gently at first, then more surely. He tasted like nuts and beer and toothpaste and heaven. She loved the feel of his lips and tongue, the way he deepened the kiss at just the right moment. She sighed with happiness and nestled closer.

He kissed her again and again until Rebecca was breathless with desire. And then he touched her, his hand closing around her breast and gently stroking.

Rebecca moaned and pressed herself closer. She forgot her admonishments to be businesslike. She forgot that she didn't want Kyle to know how much she wanted him. She forgot everything except the way he made her feel and how much she loved him.

She wanted him to go on and on, touching her, kissing her, holding her. This was what she had dreamed of for so many years. And the reality was so much better than the dreams.

He lifted her sweater. Rebecca gasped as he inserted his thumb under the lacy edge of her bra and found her nipple. The sound seemed to galvanize him, and his kiss, his seeking hand, became more urgent. Desire arched through her. All thought, all fear, disappeared, and there was only this primeval force and elemental need, as old and right as time itself.

"Rebecca, let's—"

He broke off as the doorbell rang.

They froze.

Stared at each other. His eyes asked a question, but Rebecca didn't know the answer. She looked at the door.

The doorbell rang again.

Kyle swore softly.

Rebecca pulled her sweater down. Jumped up. Who in God's name was at her door? "I'll just ignore it," she whispered, trying to calm her racing heart. Thank goodness she'd had the foresight to close the blinds. What if she hadn't? What if the visitor had looked in the window and seen them? Rebecca's face flamed as she realized what the scene would have looked like to an outsider.

Now the visitor knocked, hard.

Rebecca tiptoed to the door and peered out the peephole. JoBeth's fur-clad head was on the other side. *Oh, no, no, no...*

"Rebecca!" JoBeth yelled. "Open up. It's freezing out here, and I've got a warm pizza."

Rebecca looked at Kyle.

"I'll go in the bedroom," he said. "Try to get rid of her fast."

Rebecca waited until he was out of the room and she heard the bedroom door close before she opened the front door.

"Jeez, where *were* you?" JoBeth said. "I knew you were home. The garage is open and I saw your car." She walked straight into the living room and put the pizza down on the coffee table.

It was only then that Rebecca saw Kyle's half-finished beer. "I, uh, was in the bathroom."

"Whose car is that parked behind you?" JoBeth asked, shedding her parka and hat.

"Uh, I don't know. Probably someone visiting Mrs. Andrews." She edged her way to the coffee table. Maybe she could pick up the bottle of beer and unobtrusively take it out to the kitchen.

"That was pretty rude," JoBeth said, "blocking you in like that. What if you needed to go out?"

"Oh, I'd just call over and ask them to move it. It's no big deal. Uh, what are you doing here?"

"I was out shopping and I felt like a pizza. I know it's too early for dinner, but still . . . I've never known you to turn down pizza." She grinned, totally pleased with herself.

JoBeth lived in Moreland Hills, only a few miles away, in the house she'd gotten in her divorce decree a few years earlier. She would occasionally drop in on Rebecca, but rarely on Sunday.

Rebecca's mind raced. She considered saying she was just on her way out the door, but what if JoBeth said she'd walk out with her? How could Rebecca keep up the fiction of Jack's car belonging to a visitor of Mrs. Andrews? Thinking furiously, she picked up the bowl of cashews and the beer bottle. "Do you want something to drink with the pizza?" *Please don't notice the beer bottle.* She was already walking through the dining room on her way to the kitchen.

JoBeth followed, talking the whole time. "I could go for a beer. Boy, it was crowded in the stores today. I was looking for a new bedspread for the guest room and a gift for Sandy's baby and maybe some new boots and the only thing I found was the baby gift. I swear, I looked in ten different stores for the bedspread and couldn't find one thing I liked."

"Um, what was it you wanted?" Rebecca trashed the beer bottle and thanked her stars that JoBeth was so involved in her own concerns she'd failed to notice anything amiss. She still couldn't think how she was going to get rid of JoBeth quickly.

"I'm looking for something with jade and blue, and all I found was jade and pink or jade and mauve or jade and sea green. No blues."

Rebecca made sympathetic noises and hoped Kyle wasn't too disgusted. Oh, why did JoBeth pick today, of all days, to drop in? And why had Mrs. Andrews left the garage door open? If JoBeth hadn't seen Rebecca's car, she would probably have left after ringing the doorbell twice. God, how was she going to get JoBeth to leave?

"I thought, after we ate the pizza," JoBeth said, "you might want to go to a movie or something."

"I can't." Suddenly Rebecca knew what to say. "I have a date to meet Kyle downtown at six." She looked at her watch. "In fact, if I don't start getting ready in about thirty minutes, I'm going to be late."

JoBeth raised her eyebrows. "Meeting Kyle, hmm?"

"It's nothing like that," Rebecca said hastily. "He wanted to talk about the Mailbox account and suggested we do it over a drink and dinner. I guess he felt bad making me work on the weekend."

"Oh, darn," JoBeth said.

She looked so disappointed, Rebecca felt bad about lying to her. But it couldn't be helped. Maybe someday, when she and JoBeth were ninety-year-old women, she would tell her friend the truth and they would have a good laugh together. "I'm sorry."

"Oh, it's okay." JoBeth grimaced. "So you don't want to eat pizza, either, right?"

"I'm sorry."

"Hey, more for me. But speaking of Kyle," JoBeth said as Rebecca opened the cupboard to get a plate, "can't you just see him in L.A.? If ever a man and a city were perfectly suited to each other, it's those two.

All those big-breasted blondes and take-what-I-want attitudes. He'll fit right in. He'll leave a string of broken hearts from one end of L.A. to the other."

Rebecca cringed at JoBeth's unflattering assessment of Kyle. She prayed he hadn't heard her. "Oh, JoBeth, that's not fair."

"It's the truth, though. Hey, I know you think Kyle walks on water. I like him, too. He's a great guy. Lots of fun. But let's face it. He's selfish and self-centered." She grinned. "But then, he's a man."

Rebecca couldn't help it. She laughed and slung her arm around JoBeth's shoulders. "Come on. Your pizza's getting cold. And I've got to leave soon."

Thirty minutes later, JoBeth was finally gone.

Two seconds afterward, Kyle stormed out of the bedroom. "It's nice to know what people you thought of as your friends really think of you."

"You heard."

"What really ticks me off," he said, blue eyes blazing, "is that I'm always honest with women. I never pretend to be something I'm not, and I never lead them on or promise them anything I don't intend to deliver. If they get their hearts broken, that's their fault."

"Kyle, I'm sure JoBeth—"

"They always agree that they want exactly what I want," he continued as if he hadn't heard her. "Then they change their minds. Is that my fault?" He glared at her.

"No, of course not."

"Then, damn it, why am I labeled selfish and self-centered?"

"I don't think you're selfish or self-centered."

"I didn't hear you defending me."

"I thought the object was to get JoBeth out quickly, not engage her in a debate," Rebecca pointed out.

"Yeah, well..." His expression was glum.

"I'm sorry, Kyle," she said softly, reaching to touch his arm.

He nodded and looked away.

Rebecca tried to think of what she could say or do to salvage the situation. Her heart ached as she remembered how well things had been going before JoBeth's arrival. If only Rebecca felt confident enough to put her arms around him and try to coax him back into good humor.

"I didn't even get any pizza," he said.

Rebecca tried not to. But she burst out laughing.

To Kyle's credit, after one indignant look, he began to laugh, too.

When their laughter subsided, she said, "Um, why don't we go back into the living room and, um...try again?"

He shrugged. "Let's wait. Try again another time."

"But, Kyle, this is the exact right time of the month for me." That wasn't the only reason she didn't want to wait. She was afraid she might lose her nerve if she had to go another whole month before they tried again. "I don't want to wait."

"Well, I'm sorry, but I can't just perform on demand," he said testily. "I have to be in the right mood. And I'm *not* in the right mood now!"

Chapter Five

Rebecca pressed her lips together, and he could see she was trying not to laugh.

"I'm glad you think this is funny," he said through clenched teeth.

"I—I'm sorry," she sputtered. "I can't help it." Now she really was laughing. Hard. "I thought only women used excuses like that to avoid making love. N-never men."

He glared at her. Then he stomped to the closet, yanked it open, grabbed his jacket and without saying another word, left.

All the way home he fumed.

Damn women! They were impossible to understand. First they said one thing, then they said another. You never knew where the hell you were with them. Or what the hell they expected!

He couldn't get over Rebecca laughing at him.

She had her nerve.

Here he was, doing her a favor—a *huge*—favor, and what does she do? She laughs at him. She thinks he's funny! And just because he said he couldn't just perform on demand, like some kind of...of...*sex machine!*

He wasn't a robot.

He was a person.

He had feelings.

And JoBeth! He thought about the tone of her voice, the amusement and indulgence he'd heard when she'd called him selfish and self-centered.

He gritted his teeth.

Fine. If that's what she thought of him, fine. He personally didn't care what either one of them thought—JoBeth or Rebecca.

Maybe he'd swear off *all* women from now on.

Rebecca sat dejectedly after Kyle left. Why had she laughed at him? He'd had a perfect right to be cranky. After all, JoBeth had shown up today at the absolute worst time, making a difficult situation even more difficult. And then she'd insulted him and he'd heard. Plus he'd had to cool his heels for half an hour while he waited for her to leave, which gave him ample time to stew.

To top that off, Rebecca had been insensitive, expecting him to just pick up right where they'd left off, as if nothing had happened.

And then, when he'd balked, for a perfectly legitimate reason, she'd laughed at him.

She buried her head in her hands. *You blew it big time.*

The problem was, she'd been nervous.

She always laughed when she got really nervous.

It was a reaction to the tension, a way to let off some steam. She wouldn't blame him if he decided he had no interest in trying again. The thought that he might caused an ache in the vicinity of her heart.

No. She couldn't allow that to happen. Not only because she desperately wanted Kyle's baby, but because the taste of lovemaking she'd gotten today had shown her exactly what she'd been missing.

So no matter what she had to do or say to mend fences, she would.

Kyle was the first person in the office Monday morning. At eight o'clock, when he could hear the others arriving, he stayed put. He was ashamed of his burst of temper and his ignominious departure from Rebecca's yesterday, but he wasn't quite ready to face her with an apology. So he'd decided to skip the morning coffee ritual and plead his week-long absence from the office the previous week and the mound of paperwork waiting for him as an excuse.

Fifteen minutes later, there was a soft knock on his door. He looked up. Rebecca, a hesitant smile on her face, stood in his doorway. "May I come in?"

He gave her an answering smile. "Sure."

After she was seated in front of his desk, she said, "I owe you an apology."

"No, you don't," he said quickly.

"Yes. I do. I should not have laughed at you. I—I was nervous. I always laugh when I'm nervous." Her eyes entreated him to understand. "I'm sorry."

He could have left it at that. Allowed her to take complete blame for what had happened. She was making it easy for him. All he had to do was say, "Let's just forget about it, okay?" He was tempted. He was very tempted. Instead he took a deep breath and said, "I'm the one who's sorry. You were right. The way I acted was childish. I was ticked at JoBeth for making that crack." He hesitated, then thought *what the hell* and added, "I was nervous, too."

"Oh, Kyle..." Her smile was luminous. "I'm so glad you're not angry. I *hated* us fighting."

The thought crossed his mind that Rebecca was one heck of an attractive woman when she smiled. "I hated us fighting, too."

Then shyly, she said, "Do you want to...to try again tonight? There's, uh, only about a three- or four-day window where I'm the most fertile, and, uh—"

"I know," he cut in. "You don't have to explain. But tonight won't work. There's a board of directors meeting, and it's a very important one." Kyle had sat on the board of directors of MacNeill Department Stores ever since his grandfather had been unable to continue and had stepped down as chairman—a position Kyle's father now occupied. "But how about tomorrow night?"

"Tomorrow's fine. Thanks, Kyle." Then, her voice becoming more brisk, she said, "So tell me. What's going on with the board?"

Kyle grimaced. "Just one more attempt by my father and Julius Predlowe to sell the chain to Consolidated."

"Oh."

"Yes. Oh."

"Is there a chance they can pull it off this time?"

Kyle shrugged. "I don't know. Dad must have a majority vote. I can't imagine him making another attempt unless he's sure of the outcome this time." Kyle thought back to two years ago when his father had spearheaded the first attempt to sell off the chain and how his grandfather had thwarted him. Kyle's father had been furious, and he and Kyle's grandfather had had a terrible fight over it. Relations between them had been strained ever since, and the divorce between Kyle's parents had only added fuel to the fire.

Although Kyle wasn't interested in working in the family business himself—he was actually too much like his grandfather and needed to be in control of his own destiny—he could understand the old man's reluctance to sell out. As Graham had put it when he and Kyle had discussed the situation, "I have all the money I need. And I don't want to see MacNeill's become anonymous, just like every other big department store in the country."

"Have you tried calling the other directors?"

"Yes," Kyle said glumly. "But four of the nine were 'unavailable' and haven't returned my calls. And two of the five I did talk to told me they think selling is our best option. The problem is, the stores need another infusion of money, which means cutting into what profit margin there is. No one wants to do that. No

one except my grandfather has an emotional invest-
ment in the chain. The rest of them, including my father, see too many problems with today's competitive
retail market. They'd rather take the money and run."

"I guess you can't blame them."

"Oh, I can blame them, all right. It just won't do
me or my grandfather any good."

"Well," Rebecca said, standing, "good luck. And
now I'd better get back to work."

After she left, he turned his attention back to his
paperwork, but he couldn't concentrate. His mind
kept returning to Sunday. Not the argument he'd had
with Rebecca. And not the anger he'd felt. Now he
thought about the way it had felt to kiss her and touch
her.

Kyle had enjoyed it.

He had enjoyed it very much.

In fact, he had not wanted to stop.

He had been royally ticked off when JoBeth had so
inconveniently interrupted them.

The truth was, no matter why he'd gotten involved
in this scheme, he was looking forward to Tuesday
night.

That night, Rebecca's throat felt scratchy. She
hoped she wasn't coming down with something. She
couldn't afford to be sick. She had too much to do.

By Tuesday morning, her throat was raw and her
head ached and her nose was stuffed up. Still, she went
in to work. By noon, she knew she wouldn't last until
five o'clock. Not only was she not getting anything

accomplished at work, she was chancing infecting others in the office.

Disappointment coursed through her as she realized she would have to cancel her plans for the evening. And Kyle was not in the office. He had taken a personal day, and she couldn't reach him. He'd left her an e-mail saying the board meeting had not gone well the night before, and he had meetings with the lawyers today but he would see her about seven tonight. Rebecca had no idea which lawyers, and even if she had, she would never call him somewhere like that.

She also didn't want to leave a message with the switchboard operator at the agency. So before she left the office to go home, she called his voice mail and explained that she was sick and wouldn't be able to keep their appointment—she kind of laughed when she called it that—that night. She wasn't laughing when she realized that this postponement probably meant they would have to wait another month before there would be another prime opportunity.

Resigned, she next called her doctor and made arrangements to stop by her office on the way home.

By three o'clock she'd taken her first dose of an antibiotic and was in bed, sound asleep.

The meeting with the lawyers went on much longer than Kyle had anticipated. He debated whether he had enough time to go home and change, stop by his grandfather's house to commiserate and still get to Rebecca's by seven, but knew he didn't.

So he headed for his grandfather's. He dreaded telling the older man what he knew he must.

"I'm sorry, Grandfather," he said later. "There's no way we can block this sale."

"But dammit, Kyle!" Graham said. "This is *my* company. It's our family's company."

"I know, but things have changed." He refrained from reminding his grandfather that he'd personally made the decision to make a public stock offering twenty years earlier when he'd wanted to finance a major expansion program. Why make the older man feel any worse than he did?

"Why wasn't Donald man enough to tell me about this himself?" Graham said.

Kyle had no answer, so he didn't say anything. His father was a coward when it came to his relationship with Graham. Many men who had pulled this kind of coup in the face of opposition might have gloated and reveled in the opportunity to rub their opponent's face in it. Not Donald MacNeill. He preferred to sneak and hide. Aw, hell, maybe Kyle was being too hard on his father. Sometimes Kyle actually understood his father's feelings. Graham had pushed his son unmercifully as he was growing up, and Donald had naturally rebelled.

"I don't know what's happening to this family," Graham grumbled. "Your father, your brother, breaking up their families, and now breaking up the company. They've gone crazy."

"I'm sorry. I know this is hard."

Graham's shoulders slumped wearily. "Don't apologize. It's not your fault."

Why then, did Kyle feel as if he'd let his grandfather down? He felt even worse when, a few minutes later, his grandfather said, "Why don't you stay for dinner? Keep me company tonight."

"I can't. I've got a date. I'm sorry."

"No, no, it's okay. I understand. You go ahead. Enjoy yourself."

"Are you going to be okay?"

"Yes, yes, I'm fine. Just go on."

So Kyle left. As he drove to Rebecca's, he wondered what his grandfather would have thought if he'd known what kind of date Kyle had. *I've got an appointment to have sex with Rebecca, because she wants a baby, and I've agreed to give her one.*

Yeah, sure.

His grandfather had taken an active interest in Rebecca's life and career after she'd saved Kyle's life. Every couple of weeks, he'd ask Kyle about her, and once he'd insisted that Kyle bring her out for dinner.

Afterward, he'd hinted at how much he liked her. Finally Kyle had had to set him straight, saying, "Look, grandfather, Rebecca and I are friends. It's not that kind of relationship."

"Friends can make the best wives," the older man said. "I married my best friend."

Kyle smiled. "I wish I'd known her." His grandmother had died the year before he was born. As hoped, the mention of Julia O'Malley MacNeill effectively steered his grandfather from the subject of Rebecca.

"I wish you had, too, my boy," Graham said, his blue eyes getting that faraway look. "She was a beautiful, spirited, intelligent woman."

"Yes. I know."

"Every day of our lives together, I realized how lucky I was."

Kyle smiled fondly.

"There's nothing like a good woman to make a man's life complete."

At this point, Kyle had looked at his watch, pleaded a pressing engagement and made his escape.

No. Graham MacNeill would not be pleased with Kyle if he knew where he was headed and for what purpose.

The insistent ring of the doorbell woke Rebecca. For a moment, she was disoriented. She looked at her bedside clock, saw that it read five minutes after seven and thought it was morning.

She dragged herself up, head pounding, and walked to the front door. When she peered out the peephole and saw it was Kyle, she suddenly realized exactly what had happened.

It was Tuesday night.

And obviously Kyle had not received her message.

Fingers fumbling in her haste, she released the dead bolt and unlocked the door.

"Rebecca?" he said, his eyes sweeping her, taking in her bare feet and flannel nightgown and an appearance she was sure looked like hell. "What's wrong?"

"Oh, Kyle, I'm sorry," she said, voice thick from her cold. "I'm sick. I came home early. I left you a message on your voice mail. Didn't you get it?"

"No. I didn't."

"I'm sorry," she said again. "You've driven all this way for nothing."

By now he'd come in, bringing the cold night air in with him, and she shivered.

"Hey," he said softly, "quit apologizing. It's my own fault for not checking my voice mail." He took her arm, guiding her toward the bedroom. "You need to get back in bed."

Normally, Rebecca would have insisted she was all right. But she felt just rotten enough to like the idea of Kyle worrying about her. She meekly let him lead her to the bedroom and help her get back under the covers. He sat on the edge of the bed. "You going to be okay?"

She nodded. God, she knew she looked a wreck. Her nose was probably as red as a lobster, and her hair was probably sticking up all over.

"Did you eat anything tonight?"

"No," she croaked. She hadn't eaten anything since this morning, and then it had only been one piece of toast which she'd barely gotten down.

He stood. "You just lay there. I'm going to fix you something."

"You don't have to do that," she protested weakly.

"I know. I'm doing it anyway."

Rebecca listened to the sounds he made. The soft clunk of cupboard doors opening and shutting. The water running from the kitchen tap. The buzz of the can opener. The clink of dishes and silverware. The sounds were comforting.

About ten minutes later, he walked back into the bedroom. In his hands was a tray, and on the tray was a glass of orange juice and a bowl of soup and some white crackers to go with it.

"I'm not much of a cook," he said, smiling down at her, "but I found a can of chicken soup."

"Just what the doctor ordered," Rebecca said. She forgot how miserable she was in the face of Kyle's thoughtfulness.

He put the tray on the bedside table, then handed her the glass of juice. When she'd managed to get about a third of it down, he took the glass and picked up the bowl of soup. "Can you manage?"

Rebecca nodded.

All the while she ate, he talked. He told her about the meeting with the lawyers. Then he described his stop at his grandfather's house. And while he talked, Rebecca watched him. She loved watching him. And she loved listening to him. She loved everything about him.

"Good girl," he said when she finished the soup.

Rebecca had to admit she felt slightly better. Whether the improvement was due to the food or to the fact that Kyle had prepared it, she didn't know, but it really didn't matter. He was here. He wasn't angry about the wasted trip. And he cared enough to do something nice for her.

He removed the tray and its contents, and once more Rebecca listened to him in her kitchen. She couldn't help but imagine what it would be like to have him around all the time. What sheer bliss to wake up each morning and have his head on the pillow beside her, to share a home and a bed and a life.

Stop wishing for things you can't have....

She sighed and snuggled deeper into the covers. A few minutes later, Kyle was back. He sat on the side of the bed again. "Feeling any better?"

She smiled. "Actually, yes. Thank you, Kyle. I appreciate this."

He smiled back. Then he leaned over and kissed her cheek. "Get a lot of rest, and I'll check on you tomorrow, okay?"

"Okay."

"I'll let myself out."

"All right."

He squeezed her hand, told her again to go to sleep and then he was gone.

On the way home, Kyle asked himself what, exactly, he was doing.

Unfortunately he had no answer.

The only thing he did know was that this project of getting Rebecca pregnant, which he hadn't been in favor of to begin with, was not looking promising.

In fact, if he believed in signs, he'd say somebody up there was trying to tell him something.

Chapter Six

The only reason Rebecca managed to get through the next twenty-three days was because Kyle was gone from the office much of the time. Otherwise, the tension of waiting and thinking about the upcoming "appointment" might have proven to be too much for her to handle without alerting JoBeth, and possibly others in the office, that something wasn't quite right.

As it was, one Wednesday when they were having lunch together, JoBeth commented that Rebecca didn't seem herself these days.

To which Rebecca replied, "I'm just tired. I guess I never really got over that bout of bronchitis I had earlier in the month."

"Well, you should take better care of yourself," JoBeth cautioned. "My cousin ended up with a bad case of mono because she let herself get run-down."

Her brown eyes reflected her concern. "Are you getting enough sleep?"

"Yes," Rebecca lied, although most nights she had a hard time falling asleep because once her mind was free of the pressures and concerns of the workday, it relentlessly turned in the direction of Kyle.

"What about exercise? Exercise is extremely important when you have a sedentary job like we do."

Rebecca chuckled. "JoBeth, you're not my mother."

JoBeth smiled sheepishly. "I know, but for some reason I worry about you."

"Well, I appreciate it, but you don't have to. I can take care of myself." Her words notwithstanding, Rebecca wondered what JoBeth would think if she had any idea what was going on in Rebecca's life.

You know what she'd think. She'd think you're crazy. Well, maybe Rebecca *was* crazy, but she was committed to her course of action, and right now, all she wanted was to get it over with so she didn't have to think anymore.

Finally, the end of January rolled around, and it was once more close to Rebecca's optimum time of the month. She knew Kyle would return from a trip to L.A. the following day, a Friday. She wasn't sure if he'd make it into the office or not, so she decided to leave him a note.

Not wanting to chance another fiasco like the night she was sick, she decided to hand-deliver the note to his condominium complex on her lunch hour. She would leave it with the security guard, who would put it in Kyle's mail slot. That way, there would be no slipups. Kyle would have it the moment he set foot in the building.

In the note she told him this weekend would be the right time for them to try again, if it was convenient for him, and would he please call her on Friday after he got home.

Although the weather was cold, Rebecca enjoyed the fifteen-minute walk to the riverfront location. Kyle lived in one of the nicest condominiums, with an excellent view of the Cuyahoga River and The Flats, the renovated area bordering the river that contained trendy shops and a multitude of restaurants and clubs. In some ways, she envied Kyle for being able to live so close to the downtown action, even though she loved Chagrin Falls and its charming, small-town atmosphere.

She entered the complex, gave the note to the guard, then started the walk back to the office. On the way, she stopped at a tiny hot dog shop and bought a steaming Chicago-style hot dog and a diet drink, which she ate while standing at the counter.

As she ate, she couldn't help remembering the last time she'd been there. It had been sometime the previous September, and the weather had been gorgeous. She'd been with Kyle, and she'd gently chided him because he'd eaten two of the large hot dogs and a huge order of fries—his typical junk-food lunch.

He'd paid no attention, of course, just shrugged and continued relating a story about a customer who had been trying to give him a hard time but hadn't been succeeding. Rebecca remembered how hard he'd made her laugh and how much fun they'd had.

Suddenly she was awash in a wave of emotion so fierce, she felt stripped bare. It happened this way sometimes, this potent reminder of how much she loved Kyle. Mostly she managed to keep her feelings pushed deep inside, because complete awareness of them was too painful, bringing as it did the inevitable realization that Kyle did not share them and never would.

But you're going to have his baby, she reminded herself. *That's tons more than a lot of women have. So stop feeling sorry for yourself!*

Her little lecture enabled her to regain control of her emotions, and she finished her lunch and headed back to the office, where she managed to bury herself in work and forget about her personal problems.

The next day she wasn't quite as successful. Still, she somehow got through the day without any mishaps. Her foresight in leaving a note for Kyle at his building proved to be a smart move, as he did not make it into the office before she left at five.

She arrived home at six-thirty, having stopped to do her weekly grocery shopping on the way. She busied herself putting away the groceries, feeding and talking to Mariah, changing clothes and fixing herself some supper. She tried not to look at the clock. She also tried to pretend she was not nervous.

At eight forty-five, just as she began to think maybe Kyle hadn't returned to Cleveland that day as planned—or worse—didn't want to talk to her so was avoiding calling, the phone rang.

"Hi," he said. "I just got in and got your note." He sounded tired.

"Hi," she said, her heart giving a joyous hop. "How was the trip?"

"Productive. I'll tell you about it when I see you. I'm bushed right now."

"I thought you sounded tired."

"Yeah, I missed my flight and ended up sitting around LAX for hours before I could get on another one. Just the way you do not want to spend a Friday afternoon."

Rebecca made sympathetic noises.

"I just wanted to tell you that this weekend's fine."

"Oh. Good."

"How about tomorrow night?"

"All right." She strove to match his casual tone. "Why don't you come for dinner? Say about seven?"

"Great. See you then."

After they hung up, Rebecca stood unmoving for a long moment. Her heart pounded. Her wait was almost over.

This time, Rebecca was ready for anything. And determined that nothing would interfere with the objective of the evening.

Again, her apartment sparkled. Again, she'd closed all the blinds. Again, she'd prepared the bed and turned down the covers.

She'd also put special, low-wattage, pink-tinted light bulbs in the lamps. She'd selected several romantic CDs, which were ready to be played. She'd put a couple of bottles of wine in the refrigerator to chill. There were scented candles in each of a dozen crystal candleholders and logs in the fireplace—both waiting to be lighted at the strategic time. She'd even bought fresh flowers earlier in the day. They were arranged in two vases, one on the dining table and another on her dresser in the bedroom. Rebecca thought they looked lovely and gave the apartment just the right touch.

Dinner was prepared, too. A chicken-and-rice casserole with cheese and fresh mushrooms—mushrooms being one of the few vegetables other than lettuce and tomatoes that Kyle liked—was ready to pop into the oven, a green salad was already fixed and in the refrigerator and a loaf of French bread waited to be sliced.

For dessert, she'd made a brown Betty—another of Kyle's favorites—and the fragrant mixture of apples and cinnamon permeated the apartment.

And, the crowning touch, the black lace-and-chiffon nightgown-and-peignoir set and matching satin mules she had decided she would wear.

She'd thought long and hard about the sexy intimate apparel, which she'd purchased one day a year or so ago in a fit of hopefulness.

She knew she had presented her proposal to Kyle as a business proposition, but the fact remained that in order to grant her wish, the two of them had to engage in an intimate and very personal act. Dressing the part might help set and sustain the mood.

So she donned the nightgown-and-peignoir set and dabbed herself with cologne. She stood in front of her floor-length mirror and gave herself a critical once-over.

All right. She still wasn't beautiful, but the attractive nightwear made her look softer and more feminine. It also emphasized her curves, revealing just enough to be provocative. Her hair looked nice, too, falling in shining waves around her shoulders.

Well, that was it, she thought as she walked around, giving the apartment a last check. She'd done everything she could think of to ensure the success of the evening. The candles were all lit, the fire was burning cheerfully in the living room and the CD player was turned on.

By now, her stomach was jumping with nerves, and she kept wetting her lips and looking at the clock.

She also kept peering outside. What she saw did not reassure her. It had been snowing since noon—big, fat, heavy snowflakes that had turned the landscape into a blanket of white. And it didn't look as if it were going to stop anytime soon.

What if Kyle decided the weather looked too bad to chance driving all the way out to her place? *No, please God, don't let that happen....* She just couldn't face another postponement. Her nerves wouldn't take it. Plus she was afraid that if there was another delay, Kyle might change his mind for good.

So she mentally held her breath until the moment her doorbell rang, a good twenty minutes later than he'd said he would arrive. Relief caused her knees to feel weak, but it also helped alleviate some of her tension.

She took a deep breath and walked to the door.

Kyle's eyes widened as his gaze swept her. "Hi. I, uh... Sorry I'm late. The roads are bad."

"I figured they were." What was he thinking? Did he like the way she looked? She stepped back and he walked inside. Snowflakes clung to his hair and jacket. Her heart wrenched painfully as a wave of longing swept her. She loved him so much. It constantly amazed her that he was so oblivious to how she felt.

"That's some outfit," he said, turning to look at her again. His blue eyes held an appreciative gleam.

"Well, I thought, you know..." *Darn! Why was she stammering like some kid?*

He smiled. "I'm not objecting. I like it."

She was disgusted with herself, because she knew she was blushing. She could feel the heat staining her face and neck. "Thanks."

He took off his gloves and jacket. Underneath he wore gray wool slacks and a white cashmere sweater. He bent to remove his boots. She reached for his jacket.

"That's okay. I'll hang it up. I know where the closet is."

"Um, okay. Would you like a drink? Maybe a glass of wine or something? Dinner's almost ready." *Stop babbling, Rebecca. You sound like an idiot.*

"Wine sounds good." He hung up his jacket, then followed her back to the kitchen.

Telling herself to settle down—*he won't bite you, Rebecca!*—she removed a bottle of wine from the refrigerator. When she turned around, Kyle was so close, she nearly bumped into him. "Oh, sorry." Her heart raced as their eyes collided.

He slowly took the bottle from her. "Where's your opener?"

"I, uh, in that drawer." She pointed to the appropriate one.

He uncorked the wine, then poured some into the two glasses sitting on the counter. He smiled again as he handed her a glass. Rebecca wrapped her hand around the stem and hoped he hadn't noticed how her fingers were trembling. She sipped, her gaze again meeting his as he, too, took a swallow. Her heart was beating too hard. She was afraid he would hear it. "D-do you want to go sit in the living room? The casserole is supposed to sit awhile before serving it."

"Sure."

She moved past him carefully, avoiding contact, and walked toward the living room. She sat in her favorite chair. He sat on the couch. They sipped at their wine. The Linda Ronstadt CD ended. A few seconds later, the mellow strains of vintage Nat King Cole filled the room.

They listened to "That Old Black Magic" in silence for a while; then Kyle cleared his throat and patted the couch next to him. "Come sit by me," he said softly.

Rebecca's heart lurched. Her legs felt rubbery as she covered the short distance. When she sat down, a few inches from Kyle, he reached for her glass, taking it and placing it on the coffee table along with his own. Then he put his arm around her shoulders and tugged her closer. He gently lifted her chin. Their eyes met.

A person could get lost in his eyes, she thought. They were so blue, so incredibly blue, and so deep and clear.

"You look beautiful," he whispered.

Rebecca swallowed. She seemed to have lost the ability to speak.

He kissed her then. A soft, exploratory kiss that slowly deepened and became more insistent. The hand that wasn't around her shoulders rested against her waist, but as the kiss heated, it moved up to cup and gently caress her breast.

Rebecca's body reacted instantly, flowering to his touch. She sighed and put her arms around him. He kissed her again and again—deep, drugging kisses—then slowly his mouth moved from her lips to the hollow of her throat, to the crevice between her breasts. Rebecca reveled in the sensations storming her body. She forgot everything. The dinner waiting to be eaten. Her shyness. Her fear. All of her inadequacies. There was only Kyle. His mouth. His hands. And the awareness that he wanted her. He wanted *her*. Rebecca. These kisses were not the kisses of a man being forced to do something he didn't want to do. These kisses were the kisses of a man who desired her. The knowledge thrilled Rebecca, and she responded eagerly and passionately.

Before she even realized what was happening, he lifted her in his arms and headed for the bedroom. She kept her arms wrapped around his neck, and buried her face against his chest. Her heart thudded like crazy.

Once they were inside her candle-lit bedroom, he gently set her down. "Let's get rid of these," he said, reaching for the ribbons on her peignoir. As she slowly removed the peignoir and gown, he began to undress, too. He undressed hurriedly, letting his clothes join hers in a jumble on the floor.

In moments, they stood before each other divested of all barriers. In the flickering candlelight, Kyle looked magnificent. Before Rebecca had a chance to feel self-conscious, he pulled her into his arms and held her close. Rebecca's breath caught as he fitted her body to his. Even her imagination hadn't prepared her for the delicious intimacy of skin against skin.

His mouth captured hers again, in a long, heated kiss that stole her breath away. Eventually he lifted her to the bed and lay down beside her. His touch ignited her. Soon they were a tangle of arms and legs and seeking mouths. Rebecca felt as if she'd turned to liquid inside as his hands caressed and explored, finding every secret place that yearned to be touched. And then, just as she was sure she couldn't endure another moment of wanting him, he took her, raising himself up and entering her with one sure, swift stroke.

As he filled her, Rebecca wanted to laugh with joy. She wanted to cry. She wanted to shout.

This union felt so good, so right.

She was finally complete.

Afterward, Kyle held her close. He pulled the covers up and over them and she snuggled deep into his arms.

"Our dinner's cold by now," she whispered.

"It doesn't matter." He stroked her hair, then kissed her forehead. Soon her breathing settled into the even rhythm of sleep. Kyle closed his eyes, too, but he didn't sleep. He was too busy thinking.

He hadn't had any trouble getting in the mood tonight. The moment he'd laid eyes on Rebecca in her sexy black nightgown, he'd been turned on. In fact, he could hardly wait to make love to her.

He hadn't been disappointed, either. He'd been afraid, considering the circumstances, that they might be awkward with each other. But their lovemaking hadn't been awkward at all. In fact, it had been pretty terrific.

Rebecca had surprised him. Underneath that proper and very ladylike exterior beat the heart of a sexy, passionate woman. Her enthusiasm for their lovemaking had spurred him on and enhanced his own pleasure.

Just before he fell asleep, the thought crossed his mind that it might not be such a bad thing if it took awhile for Rebecca to get pregnant.

Rebecca awoke to darkness. She wondered what time it was. She couldn't see her digital clock unless she raised herself up, and she didn't want to disturb Kyle, so she closed her eyes again and tried to go back to sleep. But she couldn't. She was too aware of Kyle holding her, too conscious of his warm breath against her forehead, his leg nestled between hers.

She couldn't remember ever feeling this good. This happy. Being with Kyle had been so wonderful. She told herself not to get all crazy. She told herself to remember that Kyle was not in love with her. That he wouldn't even be there if she hadn't pressured him into it. Still, it was hard not to think how right this seemed—the two of them together.

She loved him so much.

If only...

Stop dreaming, Rebecca!

She sighed softly. She knew it was stupid to wish for more than she had.

Kyle stirred and mumbled something in his sleep. His arms tightened around her reflexively. Rebecca smiled. Within moments, she had fallen asleep again.

The next time Rebecca awoke, it was daylight. And Kyle was gone. She sat up, heart pounding, until she heard him in the kitchen. He seemed to be making an awful lot of noise.

She hurriedly got out of bed and scampered, naked, into the bathroom. When she emerged five minutes later, she'd washed her face, brushed her teeth and hair and put on her terry-cloth robe and slippers. The house felt awfully chilly, she thought, as she walked out to the kitchen where she found Kyle swearing softly and banging cupboards open and shut. He wore his slacks and was barefoot and bare-chested. His hair was all tousled. He looked wonderful.

"Is something wrong?"

He turned. The irritated look faded, and he smiled. "Good morning."

"Good morning."

"Yes, something's wrong all right. The electricity is out."

That's why the bathroom light wouldn't go on when she'd tried. She'd thought she just needed a new light bulb. That's also why it felt so cold in the house. Although the furnace was gas, the blower operated via electricity. "There must be a blown fuse."

"I think it's a bit more than a blown fuse," he said. "Look outside." He inclined his head toward the backyard.

Rebecca opened the back door and stepped down into the enclosed porch. She gasped. The snow came all the way up to the windows. "Oh my God," she said. "There must be four feet of snow out there."

He nodded glumly. "Yep. It must have snowed all night. You can't even see my car. It's buried. I've never seen anything like it. Go look out front. You won't believe it."

Rebecca walked down the hall and into the living room. The blinds were open and the room was flooded with light. She stared out at an unbelievable sight. There was no street, no sidewalks, no front porches visible. Everything except the top halves of the houses was buried in snow. The scene looked almost surreal. "Wow."

"Yes, wow," Kyle said from behind her. "You don't, by any chance, have a portable radio, do you?"

"Yes, I do. It's in the hall closet."

"Good. What about instant coffee? That's what I was looking for when you caught me swearing."

"I have some of those instant coffee bags. You know, like tea bags?"

"Saved," he said.

Rebecca was never so glad to have a gas stove as she was today. They brewed mugs of coffee and stood sipping it and listening to the radio. They quickly discovered they were not alone as far as the absence of electricity went. Three quarters of the city had lost electrical power due to heavy snow and ice on the lines.

"This is the worst snowfall to hit northeastern Ohio since 1951," the newscaster said. "Officials are predicting it will be three or four days, possibly more in outlying areas, for snowplows to get through. I hope our listeners have plenty of food and supplies, because it's going to be awhile before you'll be able to go anywhere."

"Three or four days!" Rebecca said.

Kyle's eyes met hers. "I had a feeling." He gave her an odd look. "I guess you're stuck with me."

Rebecca's heart gathered speed as the import of his words sank in. Kyle would be here for days, perhaps longer.

They were snowbound.

Just the two of them.

Chapter Seven

The best thing that could be said about the situation, Kyle thought as he and Rebecca ate French toast and link sausages and listened to the radio, was the fact that the weather had taken the awkwardness out of the morning after.

Instead of wondering how to act or what to say to each other, they could focus on the almost unprecedented halt to city life. They could worry, along with the radio broadcaster, about the people who weren't as fortunate as they were. They could shake their heads and look out the window and wonder when they would be reconnected to the rest of the world.

"I'm so glad you're here," Rebecca said. "It must be terrible for those people who are alone and isolated. Scary. I mean, what if something happened to them, and they couldn't get any help?"

Kyle, who had been kicking himself for the past hour, suddenly felt ashamed of his selfish thoughts. "I'm glad I'm here, too," he said softly.

"We really are lucky," she continued thoughtfully. "We won't freeze to death, and we won't starve. I just went grocery shopping yesterday, so I've got tons of food, including a full freezer. And the hot water heater is gas, so we'll have hot water." She smiled sheepishly. "And you know me. I'm such a control freak, I've got plenty of batteries, and I just had a load of firewood delivered last weekend."

She was right, he thought. It could be a lot worse. "I don't suppose you've got a snow shovel."

She laughed self-consciously. "Actually I do. It's in the basement."

Amused, he laughed, too. "You're unbelievable, you know that?"

"Well, after I'd gotten stuck once where I had to tromp through a foot of snow to get to the garage, I learned my lesson. Now I'm prepared."

He could see she was embarrassed. Tenderness flooded him, and he reached across the table and squeezed her hand. "That was a compliment."

She blushed as their eyes met. Suddenly his mind was filled with vivid images of the night before, and Kyle was chagrined to find that instead of talking about food and firewood and snow shovels, what he really wanted to do was haul her onto his lap and make love to her again. He abruptly let go of her hand, but the thought refused to go away. He remembered how soft she was and how good she felt, and he wanted nothing so much as to slip his hand between the overlapping folds of her robe and stroke the silky skin underneath. Desire, strong and almost painful, gripped him.

"Have you checked to see if the phone is working?" he said, trying to divert his thoughts. His voice sounded strained, and he hoped she didn't notice.

"No, I didn't even think of it."

"If it is, maybe you should call Mrs. Andrews and see if she's okay. And I'd like to call my grandfather." Why did she have to look so damned appealing this morning? And how was it that he'd never noticed how sexy Rebecca was?

"Mrs. Andrews isn't home. She left Friday to visit her daughter in Florida." Rebecca leaned forward and, as she did, her robe gapped open a little, exposing creamy skin and the darker crevice between her breasts.

Kyle swallowed. "Good. At least we won't have to worry about her." He stood abruptly. "I'll go check the phone." He had to get out of there before he did something he might be sorry for later.

The phone was dead.

Even so, he stayed in the kitchen for a few moments longer before walking back into the dining room. When he finally had his libido under control, he rejoined her. "The phone's out."

"Oh, dear."

"My grandfather should be okay, though. There are at least ten fireplaces in the house, and he's got plenty of firewood. And I'm sure there's a big supply of food. Hugo always keeps a lot on hand because he hates to shop. And my grandfather's not alone. That's the important thing."

"Yes. Besides, he might have electricity," Rebecca pointed out. "They said some people do."

Kyle nodded. "That's true."

They fell silent for a few moments; then Rebecca rose and began clearing off the table. Kyle immediately began to help her. Between them, they made short work of washing and drying the dishes. When they were finished, Kyle said, "Well, since we can't watch TV or listen to music or go anywhere, what do you say to a game of gin rummy?"

She cocked her head to one side. "You sure? The last time we played gin, I beat the pants off you." Her eyes sparkled in amusement. "Maybe we should try an easier game?"

"Last time I was being a gentleman."

"Meaning what? That you let me win?"

He shrugged. "Let's put it this way. I wasn't trying very hard."

She considered him for a moment, then a slow smile spread across her face. "Okay. Fine. I'll let you get away with that excuse, but be warned. It won't work again. So you'd better give today's game your best shot."

He bit back a grin. "That sounds like a dare."

"It's not a dare. It's a challenge."

"You certainly are confident."

"I'm so confident, I'm even willing to play for money."

He looked at her. At the hair that tumbled around her face and shoulders, at the sparkling green eyes, the soft mouth, the so-soft skin. He remembered the way she'd cried out during their lovemaking, how she'd felt in his arms. "Whoever wins," he said slowly, "can declare whatever winnings they want. How does that sound?"

"Dangerous," she said.

For the rest of the day, they played one game after another while listening to the radio and trying to keep warm. Although it wasn't snowing anymore, the weather remained below freezing, and it wasn't long before the house was really cold.

Luckily for Kyle, Rebecca liked oversize T-shirts and sweatshirts, and she even had a couple of big flannel shirts she'd bought in an army surplus store. "I don't suppose you've got a pair of jeans," he said hopefully.

"If you fit into my jeans, I'll shoot myself," she said. "But you can probably wear my sweatpants, because I buy them big and they've got elastic waists."

For their supper, they ate the food Rebecca had prepared the previous evening. The casserole wasn't as good as it should have been—it had sat too long the night before—but it wasn't bad.

After supper, they let the dishes soak, since the dishwasher couldn't be run without electricity. Kyle said, "Well? Want a chance to get even? Or should I declare my winnings?"

Rebecca shrugged, not quite meeting his eyes. "That's up to you."

He smiled—a slow, lazy smile—then moved closer. She was standing with her back against the kitchen counter, and he put his hands on either side of her, effectively trapping her there.

Rebecca's heart skittered at the look in his eyes. She wet her lips and his gaze followed the movement of her tongue. Desire arched through her.

"Rebecca," he said.

"Yes?" Her voice sounded like it belonged to someone else.

"We do want to make sure you get pregnant, don't we?"

All she could do was nod.

"Then what are we waiting for?"

If anything, the second time they made love was even better than the first. They took more time, for one thing. And Kyle was more playful, for another. He teased her, saying things like, "I should play gin rummy more often if this is what I have to look forward to," and they laughed a lot.

The circumstances added to their enjoyment, Rebecca felt. Huddling under the covers, the only light the flickering candles, the almost eerie silence all around them, with the absence of cars and sirens and all the background noises people take for granted.

And Rebecca felt bolder, too. She touched Kyle when he touched her and thrilled to his obvious pleasure. Later they slept entwined in each other's arms.

On Monday morning, Kyle built a big fire in the fireplace while Rebecca fixed oatmeal and bacon and experimented with toasting bread over the gas flame.

They sat on the living room floor, in front of the fire, and ate and listened to the radio again.

"County officials are concerned about elderly people living alone," the newscaster said. "If you know of anyone living around you who might be at risk, and you can reach them, please check on them."

Rebecca glanced at Kyle. He was frowning, and his eyes were worried. She touched his hand. "Don't worry. Your grandfather's all right. He's got Hugo."

He gave her a grateful smile.

The phones were still out, so they spent another day incommunicado. Wrapped in blankets, they passed the morning reading and talking. In the afternoon, they saw that one of the across-the-street neighbors had managed to push his front door open enough so that he could begin shoveling off the porch, and Kyle insisted on trying the same thing.

Between he and Rebecca, they did manage to open a big enough wedge for Kyle to try clearing a pathway. He bundled up in a double layer of Rebecca's sweats, his jacket and boots and an old knit cap of hers.

She decided to join him. Although she didn't have a second snow shovel, she improvised by taping her dustpan to her broom, and although it wasn't great, it worked well enough for her to feel she was doing something to help.

They waved and shouted to her neighbor, who waved and shouted back. "Is your phone working?" Rebecca called.

"No," he called back.

It took them a couple of hours, but they did manage to clear a two-foot-wide path to the front steps. Kyle expelled a breath and said, "That's enough for today. In the morning, I'll tackle the steps."

"Okay." Rebecca was cold, but she felt better for the exercise.

Kyle chuckled. "'Course, I don't know what good it's going to do, since the street has completely disappeared."

"Sooner or later, the snowplow will get through, and when that happens, we'll be ahead of the game," she said.

After they went back inside, Kyle built up the fire again and Rebecca fixed them hot chocolate and grilled-cheese sandwiches and tomato soup. For dessert, they finished off the brown Betty.

"That was good," Kyle said.

"Thanks."

"All that physical exertion really gave me an appetite."

"Yes. Me, too."

Silence fell between them. Rebecca thought about cleaning up but she was so comfortable and warm sitting by the fire, she hated to go into the cold kitchen. Even Mariah, who had spent most of the two previous days under Rebecca's bed—avoiding Kyle, no doubt—had come out and was snuggled down next to Rebecca.

As if he'd read her mind, Kyle said softly, "Why don't you just leave the dishes? We'll do them in the morning."

She nodded. "Good. I didn't feel like moving."

"I think we should make our bed out here tonight, in front of the fire."

Our bed. Rebecca's heart beat a little faster. "Um, okay."

Ten minutes later, they had dragged her mattress out to the living room. Five minutes after that, under the toasty warmth of their shared blankets, with the firelight flickering over them, they were making love.

Rebecca's last clear thought before she gave herself up completely to Kyle was that she hoped the snowplows never got through.

Tuesday morning brought a return of electricity.

"*Yesss,*" Kyle said. "Now I can see to shave."

Rebecca smiled. "I was going to take a shower now, but if you want to use the bathroom first, go ahead."

"That's okay. I'll wait until after you're done."

"No, really, I don't mind."

"Ladies first. I insist," he said.

"All right."

Rebecca had hated showering by candlelight and had gotten in and out quickly. But today she closed her eyes and let the hot water beat on her skin.

"Want company?"

Rebecca's eyes popped open as a gorgeously naked Kyle joined her in the shower. Afterward, she knew she would never forget the experience. In fact, she decided if she died now, she'd die happy.

If making love in bed was wonderful, it didn't compare to making love in the shower. Even the awkwardness of bumping elbows and standing up didn't diminish her pleasure and the sheer sexuality of the experience.

Afterward, they dried each other off, then Kyle lifted her into his arms and carried her back to their makeshift bed on the living room floor.

"Again?" she said.

"We want to make sure it takes," he said seriously.

Oh, yes, she would definitely die happy.

Tuesday afternoon her telephone service was restored. The first thing Kyle did was call his grandfather. His half of the conversation and his relieved smile told Rebecca everything was okay with the older man.

"He's fine," Kyle said when he hung up. "And you were right. He never lost his electricity or his phone service. He said he tried to call me. I guess he was worried about me, too."

"I'm so glad."

Then Rebecca called the office. Mark answered the phone. He told her not to worry. Only he and one of the account reps had been able to make it in that day. "Don't even try to come in before Monday," he cautioned. "Even though they're getting some of the roads cleared out, it's going to be a mess for a while."

Then Kyle called the office. "I had a date Saturday night," he said, "and I'm stuck out in the boonies." He smiled apologetically at Rebecca. "I don't know when I'll make it in."

"Sorry," he said after hanging up.

"It's okay. You *are* stuck in the boonies."

He walked over to where she was sitting, and reached for her hand, drawing her up and putting his arms around her. "I'm enjoying being stuck."

"Are you?" she said breathlessly.

He smiled lazily and kissed the tip of her nose. "Yep. Now how about another game of gin rummy? I feel incredibly lucky today."

It was Thursday morning before the temperature had risen enough to melt some of the snow and the snowplows were able to clear the roads. Rebecca's street was cleared by three. However, Kyle still couldn't go anywhere, because his car was still buried in Rebecca's driveway. But at least now they could walk downtown.

They bundled up and began clearing a path to the street. They had to quit when it got dark, but Friday morning, right after breakfast, they went back to work, and by noon there was a narrow walkway from the porch to the street.

They went inside, tired but pleased with their handiwork, had lunch, and after a short rest, decided to make the trek downtown.

Miraculously they found that some of the shops were open. Here, in the business district, the plows had cleared the sidewalks, too, and people were everywhere. Obviously everyone else in town had cabin fever, too. There were even a few four-wheel-drive vehicles on the streets.

Kyle was thrilled because one of the men's clothing stores was open, and he was able to buy two pairs of jeans and two sweaters, as well as underwear and socks, a knit hat, heavier gloves and some heavy hiking boots. He changed into his new gear before leaving the store and looked so pleased with himself, Rebecca couldn't help laughing.

They ate supper at the little Italian restaurant on the main drag, where the pizza was superb. Afterwards replete, they walked back to her apartment. Now that she had heat again, and the TV worked, they decided to watch a movie and Rebecca fixed them a big bowl of popcorn to share. After spending so many days together, they felt comfortable with each other, and Rebecca had fallen into the dangerous habit of pretending they were married and Kyle would be there always.

She knew this pretense was not only dangerous but foolish. She knew she was just setting herself up to be miserable when he was finally able to go home. She knew that probably within days he would be gone.

Still she pretended.

That night, for Rebecca, their lovemaking was bittersweet. It was still wonderful, but underlying the sweetness and pleasure was the knowledge that it would soon be over.

It was.

On Saturday the temperature rose higher and the snow started melting in earnest. Kyle spent the day outside, shoveling out the remainder of the snow on the driveway. By Saturday night, he had cleared his car and managed to get it started.

"Why don't you wait for morning before leaving?" Rebecca suggested.

"That's a good idea."

Rebecca wondered what Kyle was thinking as they ate the pork tenderloin, roasted potatoes, green beans and apple turnovers she'd prepared for their supper. He seemed preoccupied and didn't talk much, and his blue eyes were thoughtful when their gazes met.

The preoccupation seemed to intensify as the evening wore on. He helped her with the dishes, but he didn't tease her as he usually did. Afterward, he sat with her in the living room, but she could tell he wasn't concentrating on the TV program.

Finally, at nine-thirty, he said, "Let's go to bed."

His lovemaking that night was gentle, slow, thorough and incredibly sweet. And yet, he brought her to a peak of pleasure unsurpassed in any of their previous times together. Afterward, Rebecca felt boneless and completely spent. He smoothed her hair away from her face and kissed her cheek. He was silent for so long, she began to think he might have fallen asleep. And then his arms tightened around her and he whispered, "I'm going to miss this."

Then don't leave! her heart cried.

"I hope things work out the way you want them to," he added.

"Y-yes, I hope so, too." *I love you, Kyle. I love you. Can't you feel it?*

She waited, hoping, praying, but he didn't answer. Moments later, the sound of his even breathing told her he was asleep.

Kyle was ready to go at nine the following morning. He called his grandfather first and told him he was going to stop by, then smiled at Rebecca. "Well, I guess I'm off."

"Be careful."

"I will." For some reason, he felt as if he should say something more, but he wasn't sure what. He'd already told her he hoped things worked out for her and that he would miss her. What else was there to say?

Damn, but he felt awkward. Especially since she was acting so casual. He almost felt as if he should shake her hand, but that was ridiculous considering what they'd been doing for the past week. Yet her almost-standoffish attitude this morning made him feel funny about kissing her. Then he thought, oh, hell, and leaned over to kiss her cheek. "See you tomorrow."

"Yes," she echoed, "see you tomorrow."

After Kyle left, Rebecca wandered around her apartment. Everywhere she looked, something reminded her of Kyle. She knew that after the past week it would always be this way.

She would never again sleep in her bed without remembering what it had been like to have Kyle there with her.

She would never again prepare a meal without remembering what it had been like to have Kyle eating with her.

She would never again wash dishes or watch TV or listen to music without remembering this week and how they'd done all those things together.

Her emotions were chaotic. She wasn't sure how she felt. What she wished.

She still wanted Kyle's baby more than anything in the world, and yet the thought of never again making love with Kyle hurt unbearably.

Maybe I'm not pregnant. Maybe we can try again....

She told herself to stop thinking that way. That would just be delaying the inevitable, and the longer the delay, the harder the eventual outcome would be.

Because she would never have Kyle on any kind of permanent basis.

No, it would be far easier for her if she *had* gotten pregnant this week. Then she could focus on the future, on the baby... and put this episode—she refused to call it a relationship—behind her.

Where it belonged.

Chapter Eight

Rebecca dreaded Monday morning. This first day back in the office would be the hardest, she knew. If she could get through it with normalcy, she would be all right.

She told herself she could.

After all, hadn't she been hiding her true feelings for years now? If she had been able to hide her love for Kyle from him and everyone else, she should be able to do anything.

It wasn't as if anyone suspected what had happened. There would be no reason for a single soul to even have an inkling that Kyle might have been with her the previous week. So it should be a piece of cake to act the way she always acted. And no one should be the wiser.

The weather once more turned out to be a blessing, making her first day back much easier, because when Rebecca got to the office, there was so much chaos as a result of the week-long work stoppage, the ordinary routine disappeared.

The phones rang incessantly, and in between, everyone in the office had tales to tell about how they had survived the great snow-in. Even Rebecca's first encounter with Kyle wasn't as awkward as she'd feared, because it took place among several co-workers who had gathered in the kitchen and were discussing the previous week. Kyle walked in in the middle of the conversation.

"Hey, Kyle," said Dell Foley, who, like Kyle, was a senior account rep, "I hear you were stuck somewhere in the burbs all week."

"Yes," Kyle answered smoothly, "and it was my own fault, because I didn't listen to the weather report before going out that Saturday." He poured himself a cup of coffee and took a swallow, his gaze briefly meeting Rebecca's over the rim of the cup.

She gave him a casual smile of greeting and pretended great interest in the open box of doughnuts, finally selecting a lemon-filled one. Before looking up again, she managed to calm the butterflies in her stomach.

"Knowing you," Dell said, laughing, "you were probably snowbound with some gorgeous blonde." He made a face. "I, on the other hand, spent the week with two very cranky chilluns."

"What happened?" JoBeth said. "Did you have your kids for the weekend?"

"Oh, yes," Dell said, "and they were not happy campers, because, of course, we couldn't go anywhere or do anything." He grimaced. "Believe me, it was the longest week of my life. I got to the point where, if I'd heard the words *But, Daaad, what can we dooo?* one more time, I might have slashed my wrists."

Everyone laughed at his perfect imitation of a childish whine.

"Yeah, I know what you mean," said Mark's secretary, Chloe. "My kids drove me up the wall those first couple of days. I mean, no TV, no video games, no computer games. They were actually being forced to *read* and play cards." She chuckled. "Oh, and I made them clean their rooms."

"Aw, poor little tykes," JoBeth said. She winked at Rebecca.

Rebecca smothered a smile. She and JoBeth had the same opinion of Chloe's kids, who had been known to royally misbehave at company picnics and other excursions.

Dell looked at Kyle again. "I'm still waiting to hear about Kyle's week."

"What?" Kyle said. "I was snowbound, like everyone else."

"Yeah, but *you* were with a gorgeous babe, right? What was she, a blonde or a redhead?" Dell said.

Kyle gave him a lazy smile. "Gee, Dell, it's so much more fun to keep you guessing."

"Drooling, you mean," Dell said morosely.

Rebecca joined in the good-natured laughter, but she avoided Kyle's gaze. She wondered what these people would say if they knew where Kyle had been. What he had been doing. What *she* had been doing. *Stop thinking about it. Before you know it, you're going to be blushing.*

Someone else said something, and the talk soon veered away from Kyle. Rebecca used the opportunity to say, "Well, I've got work to do," and headed back to her office.

JoBeth followed her. "So how'd you spend your week?" she asked, perching on the edge of Rebecca's desk.

"Oh, reading, sleeping, watching TV once the electricity was restored. How about you?"

"The same. It was kind of nice, even though by the fourth day I was a little stir-crazy."

"I know," Rebecca said, although she would have been happy to spend months cut off from the world if it had meant Kyle would be there with her.

JoBeth grinned. "Can you believe that Kyle? Even in the worst blizzard this city has ever seen, he manages to turn it to his advantage."

"Meaning?"

JoBeth rolled her eyes. "Oh, come on, Rebecca, even you aren't *that* naive. Meaning he spent the week shacked up with his latest girl-find."

Rebecca winced inwardly at JoBeth's choice of words. "We don't know that. But even if he *was* with a woman, it wasn't his fault he got stranded," she pointed out.

"Maybe not, but the outcome will be the same."

"I don't understand. What outcome?"

"Another notch on his belt, that's what outcome. I mean, you know as well as I do that every woman he's ever dated has fallen for him. All that boyish charm just gets 'em. So whoever this latest one is, after a week with Kyle, she's certainly a goner." JoBeth shook her head. "I feel sorry for her. I feel sorry for any woman who falls for Kyle. She's just asking for trouble."

Rebecca decided the wisest course was to let this remark pass, even though she was beginning to get a bit tired of JoBeth's constant criticism of Kyle. It was as if JoBeth had a personal ax to grind. Suddenly the strangest thought hit her. Had JoBeth, at one time or another, fallen for Kyle herself? Was that what was behind her negative feelings toward him? The thought stunned Rebecca, and yet, if it was true, it would explain so much.

"Well," JoBeth said, rising, "I'd better haul my butt back to my office if I hope to ever get caught up."

"Yes. I'd better get to work, too." Now that the idea had formed, it refused to go away. Rebecca eyed her friend speculatively, wondering if behind the outwardly frank exterior, JoBeth was harboring a secret, too.

After JoBeth left, Rebecca told herself she was being silly. JoBeth didn't have a secretive bone in her body. Hadn't she told Rebecca all about her marriage and divorce? Just because Rebecca found Kyle irresistible did not mean JoBeth had, too.

Kyle couldn't stop thinking about Rebecca and about how much he'd enjoyed being with her over their snowbound week. He had always enjoyed her company, but a week of enforced togetherness was a whole other story. With many friendships, having to spend a week in close confines, cut off from the outside world, might completely ruin the relationship.

But that hadn't happened with her. If anything, with each passing day, he'd become more comfortable and relaxed around her. She was very easy to be with. He kept remembering how much fun they'd had. How pleasurable it had been to share the housekeeping chores, the meals, the long conversations and the endless games of gin rummy.

And the sex... Don't forget the sex....

As if he could.

He still couldn't get over it. To think he'd wondered if he would enjoy making love to Rebecca. He'd more than enjoyed it. The experience had been... remarkable.

She had been remarkable—passionate, sexy and completely responsive. He had found himself wanting to make love to her again and again.

He *still* wanted to make love to her.

The thought troubled him.

He and Rebecca did not have a romantic relationship. And they weren't going to have one. She'd been very clear about what she wanted, and it wasn't romance. Getting pregnant was her objective. Her *only* objective.

And he certainly wasn't looking for a romantic entanglement. Especially not with someone like Rebecca. In fact, up until now, he had always thought Rebecca was a wedding-ring, picket-fence kind of person. Kyle couldn't imagine her in any sort of intimate relationship unless she figured it was going to lead to a permanent commitment.

Kyle did not want a permanent commitment.

He particularly did not want marriage.

All of this being the case, he sternly told himself to put the past week and its events out of his mind. To put making love to Rebecca again out of his mind.

He also couldn't seem to stay away from her. Over the next few days, no matter how many times he told himself not to, he found himself making excuses to go into her office. He just wanted to see her, to hear her voice.

He knew this behavior was dangerous, yet he seemed powerless to change it. He was bewildered by his conflicting emotions. If he didn't know better, he would actually think he might already be emotionally involved—*romantically* involved—with her.

No way.

Not possible.

It was just that Rebecca was his friend. He cared about her. That's why he wanted to be around her. Because she was important to him, and he wanted to be sure *she* was all right with their situation.

Yes. That was the explanation. He wanted to show her, by his continued friendship, that he was there for her. That nothing had changed between them. That nothing *would* change between them.

He owed her that much.

Rebecca's period was late.

She decided not to get excited. She was only late by

a couple of days. It was too soon to be sure about anything, because even though she was rarely late, it was still entirely possible that her period would start at any moment.

So she waited.

She was grateful Kyle was away again. She was afraid, if he were there, she might give away her inner tension.

When a week had gone by, and she still hadn't started her period, she decided she would give herself a home-pregnancy test. She stopped at the pharmacy on her way home that night and bought a test kit.

It came out positive.

Rebecca's heart pumped faster as she looked at the results of the test. Was she *really* pregnant? These tests were supposed to be pretty accurate.

She pressed her fingers against her stomach and told herself not to count on anything until she'd seen a doctor. She knew that, at the most, she couldn't be more than a few weeks pregnant.

Waiting until the middle of March was excruciatingly hard. But finally the day of her doctor's appointment arrived.

"Well, Rebecca. You're definitely pregnant," Dr. Carrington said, stripping off her disposable gloves and smiling down at Rebecca.

A plethora of emotions assailed Rebecca. Foremost was elation. It had actually happened. She was actually pregnant with Kyle's baby. But mixed with the joy was an aching sadness, because this moment, which should be the crowning moment in any woman's life, was tinged with the knowledge that Kyle would never be a part of her baby's life.

Think about what you do have, not what you don't have, she told herself sternly.

"I'm sure you have questions. But why don't you get dressed?" Dr. Carrington said. "Then come into my office and we'll talk."

"All right." After the doctor left the examining room, Rebecca squeezed her eyes shut. *Thank you, God. Thank you.*

Fifteen minutes later, seated across the desk from the doctor, Rebecca was calmer, more able to savor the happiness of knowing her heart's desire would soon come true.

The doctor told her about taking her vitamins, eating right, keeping up her exercise program—"As long as it's not too strenuous"—and recommended a book about what to expect throughout her pregnancy. "It'll answer so many of your questions."

Rebecca smiled tremulously.

"I'd estimate your due date at the end of October. Let's say October 30," Dr. Carrington said.

Rebecca's smile expanded. Her child could have a Halloween theme for his or her birthday parties. Rebecca had always loved Halloween.

"Because you're almost thirty-five, you might consider having an amniocentesis when you're about four months pregnant," the doctor continued.

Rebecca frowned. "Why? Do you think there's a problem?"

"No. But the test can tell you if there are any abnormalities—in particular, Down's syndrome—which is always a risk when a woman has her first baby in her middle to late thirties.''

"But even if there *were* abnormalities, I would still want the baby, so I don't see the point in having the test." In her heart, Rebecca knew this baby would be fine and healthy and that she would carry it to term. It was Kyle's baby. How could it not be wonderful?

"It's your choice, of course. I just wanted you to know what your options are."

"I appreciate your telling me, but I'm really not at all worried."

Dr. Carrington leaned back in her chair and studied Rebecca thoughtfully. "Rebecca, I've known you for what, two years now?"

"Yes. About that."

"So I know you're not married."

Rebecca's gaze didn't waver. "No."

"You seem happy about the pregnancy, though."

"I *am* happy. I've wanted a child for a long time. This...this was a planned pregnancy."

The doctor nodded thoughtfully. "Will the father be involved in raising the baby?"

"No."

"I see." Dr. Carrington sighed. "It's not easy raising a child alone. Believe me, I know. But I suppose you've thought of all that. You seem like an extremely sensible young woman."

"Yes, I have thought about it." Rebecca leaned forward. "Look, Dr. Carrington, I have a good job, a stable life and a really supportive family. I'm not worried. In fact, I'm excited."

The doctor smiled. "Good. Then I'm happy for you. All right. That's about it. I'll see you again in a month."

Rebecca didn't remember driving home. She knew she must have, because she arrived there, but the drive itself was lost in dreams of the baby that would arrive in seven months. It wasn't until she'd pulled into the driveway that she remembered the book Dr. Carrington had recommended. Laughing at herself, she decided she would go inside, change clothes, then walk to the little bookstore in downtown Chagrin Falls.

"What to Expect When You're Expecting," the saleswoman said later. "Yes, of course, I know the book." She showed Rebecca where to find it.

It gave Rebecca the oddest feeling to look at the cover and imagine herself wearing maternity clothes in a few months' time. She paid for her purchase and walked outside into the windy March day. Watery sunshine speckled the sidewalk and passing pedestrians, and the wind whipped at Rebecca's long coat. She was oblivious. It might have been the middle of August for all she cared.

Slowly, still half-dazed, she walked toward the Falls and the small park surrounding the shallow end. She sat on one of the benches bordering the park and dreamed about the years to come. Maybe she would use the last of her share of money from her family's business to buy a small house. She imagined what it would be like to spend Saturday mornings walking downtown with her baby in a stroller as she'd seen other mothers doing.

She refused to let her mind dwell on the fact that many of those mothers had been accompanied by smiling fathers.

I'll do just fine on my own, she told herself fiercely. *This is what I wanted. I can do this by myself.*

For the first time since Dr. Carrington had confirmed her pregnancy, Rebecca thought about breaking the news to Kyle. How would he react? She stared out over the water. If only...

Don't do this, Rebecca. Stop that thought right there.

She inhaled deeply and stood up. She would tell Kyle her news matter-of-factly and thank him for granting her her wish. She would set the tone, and he would gratefully follow it. There would be no messy emotions displayed, no expectations of anything more than he had agreed to.

She owed him that much.

Kyle returned to Cleveland the last week of March. He felt very good about this latest trip to L.A. He'd leased the perfect office space and started the ball rolling to find an office manager with an estimated start date of June 15.

He'd also called on several leads and a couple of those looked promising for future business. All in all, a very satisfying trip.

He'd missed Rebecca, though, and felt ridiculously happy about seeing her again. On the flight back, he wondered if she'd have any news for him. For her sake, he hoped she was pregnant. For his sake, he wasn't sure what he hoped.

He got to the office early the next morning. At 8:10, following his normal pattern, he got up, went to the kitchenette, filled his coffee mug, then headed for Rebecca's office. She didn't hear his approach, so he had a chance to study her for a moment without her being aware of his scrutiny. She looked exactly right, as always, in a trim burgundy wool suit and pale blue blouse. Her head was bent over her work.

He knocked softly.

"Kyle," she said, looking up with a smile. "You're back."

"Yeah, got back last night."

"Come in. Close the door."

He took one look at her shining eyes and knew what she was going to say.

"I'm pregnant," she said softly once he was seated.

He stared at her. At her bright eyes, her familiar face, her obvious happiness.

Pregnant.

Rebecca.

Pregnant.

For the first time, the word took on meaning.

Rebecca was carrying his child.

His child.

He was going to be a father. The knowledge thundered through him, leaving the oddest sensation in its wake—a mixture of disbelief, happiness and awe. He was suddenly seized by a powerful desire to pull her into his arms and kiss her.

He fought against his chaotic emotions, forcing himself to smile. He spoke carefully, with a lightness he did not feel. "That's great. We should go out for dinner tonight to celebrate. You free?"

"I— Yes, I'm free."

"Want to go to Angelo's? Or somewhere different?"

"Let's go to Angelo's."

"Okay." He stood, needing to get out of there, needing to get to the privacy of his office where he could digest this news in private. "What do you say we plan to leave here about five-thirty? That way we can get you home early." He smiled. "Don't pregnant women need lots of rest?"

"Oh, don't worry. I'm getting plenty of rest. But five-thirty is fine."

Kyle walked back to his office in a daze. His feelings bewildered him. He had never expected to feel anything other than pleased for Rebecca if she achieved her goal of a pregnancy.

"Kyle?"

"Huh?" He looked up to see Chloe standing by his office door with a puzzled expression on her face.

"Boy, you were really concentrating hard," she said. "I spoke to you twice and you didn't even hear me."

"Oh, sorry. What did you say?"

"I said I put the Cleghorne contract on your desk. Mark said you wanted to look it over."

"Thanks."

"Sure." Her brown eyes were curious. "Is something wrong?"

"No."

"You sure?"

"Of course I'm sure," he said, his voice sharper than normal.

She shrugged. "Okay."

After she walked down the hall, Kyle knew he'd better get it together. The last thing he wanted was for people in the office to think something was wrong.

And after all, nothing was wrong.

Nothing at all.

Chapter Nine

Rebecca walked over to her office window and stared out. From her vantage point, she had a clear view of a silvery blue Lake Erie, the Rock and Roll Hall of Fame and Museum on Lakeshore Drive and E. 9th Street, Municipal Stadium—which Clevelanders now called "The Mistake on the Lake"—and City Hall, with its controversial big pink FREE stamp adorning the grounds.

Normally, these were sights that made her smile. Sights she had come to love. Sights that made her feel a part of the rejuvenated city its citizens were so proud of.

Today, the familiar landmarks moved her not at all.

Today, she felt only an aching sadness and disappointment as she stared out the window and contemplated her situation.

She couldn't get over Kyle's reaction to her news. He had been so unmoved. So blasé, even. He'd treated her pregnancy as if it were no more important than landing a new client or getting a raise.

That's great. We should go out for dinner tonight to celebrate.

His words, which on the surface, seemed appropriate enough, even nice, had been delivered with such nonchalance. *That's great.*

What kind of reaction was that?

He hadn't asked her anything. Not what the doctor had said. Not when the baby was due. Nothing.

It was as if he had no interest at all. As if this baby had nothing to do with him.

She was going to have his *baby,* for heaven's sake. Didn't that *mean* anything to him?

Rebecca swallowed against the lump in her throat. *What did you think? That he'd leap for joy? Tell you he's been blind? That he loves you and wants to marry you and help you raise the baby?*

Tears filled her eyes.

Of course.

That's exactly what she'd thought.

Despite everything she'd said. Despite everything she knew. Despite all indications to the contrary, that's the reaction she'd secretly hoped for.

Oh, God, you are such a fool.

She fished a tissue out of her suit pocket and carefully blotted her eyes. Even in her misery, she was mindful of the need not to smear her mascara, not to give away, by even the tiniest clue, her fragile emotional state. An office was like a small town. People noticed everything. Gossiped about everything. And even though Rebecca knew the people in her office cared about her, she still did not want to be the object of speculation, gossip or—worst of all—pity.

Well, Kyle's reaction had accomplished one thing. At least now she knew better. Now that last faint hope that Kyle would have a miraculous change of heart was finally laid to rest. He would never want to marry her. She must accept that. She *would* accept that.

Thank God, in another month or so he would be in L.A. permanently. And in the meantime Rebecca would make sure she put on her best acting face. Because, now more than ever, it was imperative that she say or do nothing to make him suspicious about her true feelings.

Her resolve strengthened as the day drew to a close. And by the time Kyle came to her office at five-thirty, smiling and saying, "You ready?" she was in steely control of her emotions.

"Let me just put these papers in my briefcase."

Five minutes later they were on their way.

Rebecca was determined to act just the way she used to act before her proposition to Kyle. To that end, she chattered about an account he had worked on before the L.A. job came up. To her relief, he responded like the Kyle of old, and Rebecca even managed to forget, for a little while, that their relationship was irretrievably changed.

"Paul Roper actually *said* that?" Kyle said.

"He not only said it, he repeated it."

Kyle whistled. "That guy's tough." Laughing, he added, "But he met his match when he met you."

Rebecca smiled. She was proud of the way she'd handled the customer. She was also proud of the outcome. Alonzo & Christopher hadn't lost the account, which Mark had been afraid might happen. It meant a lot to her that, when it was obvious the customer wasn't happy with the progress of his account, Mark hadn't pulled her off and put someone with more experience in charge. "Thanks."

"You're welcome."

They continued to discuss business until they reached the restaurant. But once inside, after having exchanged pleasantries with Angelo and his staff and placing their drink orders, Kyle said, "I've been thinking about what you told me earlier. You know, about the, uh, baby." His eyes looked very blue as they met hers.

"Have you?" *Not as much as I have, I'll bet.* To give herself something to do, she sipped at her water.

"Yes. There, uh, were some things I wanted to ask you."

"All right." He was obviously uncomfortable.

"Have you seen a doctor yet?"

"Yes. Earlier this week."

"And he confirmed the . . . pregnancy?"

Rebecca smiled. "*She* confirmed the pregnancy, yes."

Kyle smiled, too, and when he did, some of the constraint left his voice. "I stand corrected."

"You're forgiven."

"Did the doctor say everything is okay?"

"Yes, everything's fine."

It pleased her that Kyle was concerned. Maybe he *did* have some feelings about the baby.

He nodded and seemed about to say something else, but just then their waitress brought their hot bread sticks and drinks—red wine for Kyle, iced tea for Rebecca. When the waitress walked away, he smiled and raised his glass. "Congratulations."

They clinked glasses and Rebecca slowly drank some of her tea. She tried not to think what it might be like to be celebrating this event with a husband who loved her and who was as excited about the birth of his first child as she was. *Be happy with what you have. Stop wishing for more.*

After a while, Kyle said, "Did the doctor give you a due date?"

"Yes, she did. October 30."

His eyes widened. "You're kidding."

"No. Why?"

"October 30 is my grandfather's birthday."

Rebecca smiled in delight. "Really?"

He nodded slowly.

Rebecca wondered what he was thinking. He had the strangest expression on his face. If she hadn't known better, she might have defined it as something approaching regret.

"Are they usually accurate in their predictions?" he finally asked.

"Most of time they're pretty close. I know my sister-in-law Clem was told her twins would be born March 23, and they arrived on March 22. Same way with my sister-in-law Miranda. They gave her a due date of April 3, and she only missed it by ten minutes. Robin was born just after midnight on April 4.''

By now their salads had come, and for a while they ate quietly. Rebecca decided the ball was now in Kyle's court. If he wanted to continue to discuss her pregnancy, fine. If not, that was fine, too. He now knew all the pertinent details. She still couldn't figure out what he was thinking. The only real emotion he'd shown had been when she'd told him the baby's due date.

That really *was* the nicest coincidence, she decided. Even though, after the baby arrived, she and Kyle would not have any but the most casual contact via their work, if their child was born on his grandfather's birthday, Kyle would always remember the date. Still, she couldn't help feeling sad that his grandfather would never know about his first great-grandchild.

But at least one day, when her child was old enough to start asking questions, she could be truthful in telling him or her about his or her heritage.

Even though she would not break her word and divulge Kyle's identity to anyone and would maintain the fiction of artificial insemination, even to her child, she could tell the complete truth about Kyle's background and family. That was the kind of information that would be given to any woman who was artificially inseminated.

She wondered if her baby would look like Kyle. She studied him covertly. He was so handsome, but it was his personality rather than his looks that appealed to her most. She loved the mischievous boyishness that was such an integral part of his charm.

But more than that, there was a warmth and sweetness about Kyle that made a person feel good to be around him, and the fact that these qualities were completely genuine made him irresistible.

A few minutes later, Kyle started to talk about his latest trip to L.A., and for the rest of the evening the subject of the baby was avoided.

It wasn't easy for Rebecca to push those thoughts to the back of her mind. Right now, her pregnancy was the most important thing in her life, and she would have liked to be able to discuss it if she felt like doing so. She hated having to be on guard every moment, having to watch every single thing she said for fear she would say something that would make Kyle uncomfortable, or worse, reveal emotions she didn't want him to know about.

Kyle's conversation seemed guarded, too, despite the fact that he talked easily and laughed often. There was something—some reserve—at the back of his eyes, and Rebecca knew he was feeling some of the same strain she felt.

When dinner was over, Rebecca was relieved. No matter how much she cared for Kyle, she realized that this new constraint between them would not go away. Things had changed, and the change was permanent.

Kyle paid the check and helped her with her coat. Then they walked outside.

The late-March weather was still cold, but it was a beautiful, clear night with very little wind. Rebecca breathed deeply and looked up. The indigo sky was studded with stars and a brilliant quarter moon.

"Nice night, isn't it?" he said.

"Yes."

He unlocked the car and helped her in. Their hands touched briefly, and Rebecca was disgusted to find that even that momentary contact was enough to hollow out her stomach. While he walked around to his side of the car, she told herself to be strong. She only had to make it through the next ten minutes, then she could finally relax.

When they reached Van Aken Boulevard, Kyle insisted upon walking her over to her car.

"Thanks for dinner," she said, stopping by the driver's-side door. "I really enjoyed it."

"It was my pleasure."

She unlocked her door, and he held it open while she slid inside the car. "Are you going to be in the office on Monday?" she asked.

"For a little while. My flight back to L.A. isn't until eleven-thirty."

"I guess I'll see you then."

"Yes." He leaned down and kissed her cheek. "Be careful driving home. And lock your doors."

"I will." She didn't trust herself to meet his gaze. "Good night. Thanks again."

"Good night."

She expected him to walk back to his car, but he didn't. He stood there watching as she put her key into the ignition, and she realized he intended to wait until she was safely on her way. His thoughtfulness warmed her. She turned the key.

Nothing happened except for a clicking noise. "Oh, no." She turned it again. Still only the ominous clicking. She opened the door.

"Sounds like your battery is dead," he said.

"That's what I was afraid of."

"Let's try jumping it. I've got jumper cables in my trunk."

Five minutes later, her motor was running.

"You're going to have to get someone to look at that battery tomorrow," he said.

"I will."

"In the meantime, I think I'd better follow you home."

"Oh, you don't have to do that!"

"Yes, I do. What if you get stuck? It's dangerous enough for a woman to be driving alone at night. And with as weak a battery as you seem to have, your car might stall. Then what would you do?"

She couldn't argue with his reasoning. But she could kick herself for not getting a cellular phone. She'd been thinking about it, but just hadn't acted on the idea. If she had one, she wouldn't have to inconvenience him. Well, she'd get one over the weekend. Because Kyle was right. It *was* dangerous for a woman driving alone at night, no matter where she was driving. There was no such thing as a good neighborhood anymore. And she no longer had just herself to think about. She had a precious new life inside her. She had to be doubly careful.

"You're right," she said.

All the way from Van Aken Boulevard to her duplex, Rebecca was conscious of Kyle's car behind her.

Of Kyle taking care of her. Once more, her traitorous mind veered off in the direction of how nice it would be to have him taking care of her always. And once more, she sternly told herself to stop thinking that way, because it was never going to happen. *You're just prolonging the agony.*

When they got to her place, he pulled up behind her in the driveway, then walked her to her back door.

Rebecca started to say thank-you again. Then, suddenly, she knew there was something else that needed saying. Something she should have already said.

She took a deep breath and looked up into his eyes. "Before you go, there's something I need to tell you."

"Okay."

"I've been thinking about this for days, and I, well, I just want you to know that you've made me very happy. I'll never forget it, and I . . . I'll never forget you." The last part was barely a whisper, but she managed to say it without stumbling.

For a moment, he said nothing, and then, saying only "Rebecca," he took her completely by surprise, and drew her into his arms.

Until the moment his lips met hers, she hadn't known how much she needed this, how much she needed him. She wrapped her arms around his neck and kissed him back with a fierce outpouring of all the emotions she had been hiding for so long. He kissed her deeply and passionately, and the desire that he had unleashed during the week they'd spent together ignited again.

I love you, I love you. . . .

When the kiss finally ended, she wanted him so badly, she was trembling inside.

"I'm glad I was able to give you what you wanted so badly," he whispered, his forehead resting against hers.

Please, please don't leave.... If only she had the courage to say the words out loud.

Kyle fought to control his breathing and his emotions. He knew he shouldn't have kissed her, at least not like that, but her words had touched him in a way that made him forget all reason.

And now he didn't want to leave her. He knew it wasn't smart. He knew he should say goodbye and go home. But he didn't want to. He wanted to go inside and take her to bed. He wanted to kiss her again and again and make love to her, slowly. He wanted to touch her stomach where the baby they had made together was protected as it grew to term. He wanted to hold her and talk about the future.

You can't, he thought. *You can't. The two of you don't have a future. You're going to go your way, and she's going to go hers.*

Stoically he kissed her cheek, hugged her briefly, then made himself say, "Good night, Rebecca."

"Good night," she murmured. Her head was bent.

"Call me tomorrow if you need help with your car."

"Okay."

He wished he could tell her how he was feeling, but it wasn't fair to her to indulge himself. They had a deal. He needed to abide by it. Anything else would make things harder for her.

So he said nothing as she unlocked her door and went inside. He waited until he heard the sound of the lock before walking slowly back to his car.

Kyle didn't spend much time in Cleveland during the month of April. He was too busy hiring staff and making preparations to open the Los Angeles office. He did try to stay in touch with Rebecca by phone, calling her a couple of times a week, but their conversations were less and less satisfactory to him.

It was hard to put his finger on just what was wrong. She was friendly enough, but there was a distance in her voice that was off-putting. And she was no longer forthcoming about herself. She answered his questions, but she volunteered very little on her own. If he wanted to know how she was feeling or what was happening in regard to her pregnancy, he had to ask. And then, when he did ask, she seemed guarded in her replies.

"Have I done something to make you angry?" he said one day after a particularly unsatisfactory conversation.

"No. Of course not," she replied quickly.

Too quickly, he thought. "Then why are you acting this way?"

"What way?"

"Come on, Rebecca. Don't play dumb. You know what way. You're so damned distant when we talk, I might as well be talking to a stranger. I'm getting the feeling you don't want to talk to me at all."

There was silence for a long moment. Then an audible sigh. Her voice, when she replied, was warmer and sounded more like the Rebecca of old. "I'm sorry. I never meant to give you that impression. I guess it's just . . . well, I'm not sure how to act anymore."

"Why can't you just act the way you always have?"

"Because . . ." Another sigh. "Because things have changed."

"But we're still friends. That hasn't changed."

"No," she said slowly. "No, that hasn't changed."

But something in her voice told him it *had* changed, yet he knew if he questioned her further, she would deny it. If he were talking to her face-to-face, where he could see her eyes and her expression, he might have pursued the subject, but he knew he would get nowhere on the telephone. Frustrated, he told her he had to go and he would talk to her in a day or two.

After they'd hung up, he thought about what she'd said and the way she'd said it, and he decided that the next time he was in Cleveland, he would talk to her about this again.

Rebecca thought about the conversation with Kyle again and again in the weeks that followed. She knew he wasn't happy with her replies to his questions, but what else could she have said without giving away too much of what she was feeling? If only she could have been completely honest with him, but she couldn't.

He hadn't brought up the subject again, and for this she was grateful. For her part, in all subsequent conversations, she'd tried very hard to act normal and cheerful and friendly.

Today would be the true test, though. It was Friday of the second week of May, and Kyle was coming to

Cleveland for the weekend. Rebecca knew he planned to drop by the office sometime late that afternoon.

At four-thirty, he knocked on her door. As usual, when she looked up to see him standing in her doorway, her stupid heart refused to beat in a normal pattern. But outwardly, Rebecca managed to smile and say hello cheerfully and casually. "You made it," she said as he walked in, closing her door behind him.

"Yes."

Rebecca studied his face. He looked tired. Or worried. "Is something wrong?"

"Hugo called me last night. I guess my grandfather's not been feeling well lately."

"Oh, dear, I hope it's nothing serious."

"I don't know whether it is or not. I'm going to try to convince him to see the doctor. You know how he is."

Rebecca did know. Kyle had told her once how his grandfather seemed to have a morbid fear of doctors and hospitals. "Maybe it's because of my grandmother and the way she died," Kyle had explained.

"Anyway," Kyle said now, sitting on the edge of her desk, "I'll do my best." He smiled down at her. "So how have you been?"

She returned his smile and tried not to think how much she loved him, because if she thought it, it might show in her eyes. "Fine."

"Feeling good?"

"I'm feeling wonderful."

"You're looking wonderful," he said softly. His eyes studied her approvingly.

At his praise, something warm and silky curled into Rebecca's stomach, and all the constraint that she'd been feeling momentarily slid away. She knew he was right about the way she looked. Pregnancy agreed with her. Even she, who had always been so critical of her appearance, could see the changes. Her skin looked rosier, her eyes brighter, her hair shinier. Several of her co-workers had commented on how well she looked, and Rebecca had smiled and thanked them and hugged her delicious secret to herself. She had decided she would not tell anyone about her pregnancy until she was showing enough to wear maternity clothes. "Thank you."

"Told anyone yet?" he asked quietly.

Rebecca shook her head and explained about wanting to wait. "Probably by the end of May I'll have to."

"What about your family?"

Rebecca grimaced. "No. I have to admit, I'm being a little cowardly about telling them."

He frowned. "Are they going to be upset?"

"No, not exactly." She sighed. "Well, maybe at first. But they'll be supportive. I know they will. It's just that... artificial insemination is, well, radical. I thought I might wait until after my ultrasound."

"You'll let me know if there are any problems, won't you?"

"If you want me to."

"Why wouldn't I want you to?"

She met his gaze levelly. "Well, we did agree that you would have no responsibility—"

"That doesn't mean I'm not concerned."

"All right. Then of course I'll let you know."

"Good."

For a moment, silence fell between them. "Things settled down with the new office?" Rebecca said, because they hadn't talked much since the grand opening.

"Yes. I'm really pleased with the people we've hired, especially Margaret."

Margaret Frostwood was Kyle's office manager, and he'd been bragging about her ever since snagging her away from a rival agency. Rebecca might have been jealous, except she knew Margaret was in her mid-fifties and a grandmother several times over.

"I think we're going to give the New York office a run for its money," Kyle said.

"That'll make Simon and Mark happy." Their eyes met again. "And you? Do you like it out there as much as you thought you would?"

He shrugged. "Sure. What's not to like? Sunshine, palm trees, the ocean, the mountains..."

Beautiful women... "Paradise on earth," she said lightly, resolutely pushing the image of all those California beauties out of her mind.

He smiled, but the smile seemed a little forced. Or maybe that was just wishful thinking on her part.

"Yeah, paradise on earth. Well," he said, standing, "I'd better shove off. I've got to meet with Mark, and I'm supposed to be at my grandfather's by six."

"Tell him I'm thinking about him."

"I will."

"And have a nice weekend."

"You, too."

He seemed to hesitate, and Rebecca wondered if he was going to suggest seeing her this weekend. She hoped not. This meeting had gone well, but it was playing with fire to spend too much time in Kyle's company, and she knew it. Relief flooded her when he said nothing more, just waved and left her office.

After he'd gone, Rebecca thought about the things that had been said and the things that hadn't been said. All in all, this encounter had been so much easier than the previous ones, it made her think that maybe, just maybe, she was getting over him.

She hoped so.

It was certainly about time.

Chapter Ten

On Tuesday of the following week, Rebecca was
scheduled to have her first ultrasound with a radiologist. Once it was underway, the doctor said, "Do you
want to know the sex of your baby?"

"Yes," Rebecca said eagerly. "I do."

"Look." He pointed to the ultrasound picture. "See
there? That's the baby's head. Now watch. There. See
that? It's very definitely a boy."

Rebecca's eyes filled with tears as she stared at her
baby. He was moving. And she could hear his little
heart beating. It was the most unbelievable feeling to
actually see him there, inside of her, growing and
waiting to be born. *Oh, Kyle, if only you could see our
son. The baby we made together. Surely then...*

"He looks good," the doctor said. "Strong and
healthy."

The nurse in attendance smiled at Rebecca, and Rebecca, pushing away her thoughts of Kyle, gave her a tremulous smile in return.

For the rest of the week, Rebecca hugged her knowledge to herself, savoring it and getting used to it. But by Friday she decided it was time to announce her pregnancy. She had known she would have to, and very soon, because she could no longer button the waistband of her skirts. And now that she even knew the baby's sex, there was no longer any reason to wait.

Smiling, she picked up her phone and buzzed Jo-Beth's office.

"JoBeth Weaver."

"Hi, J.B. Do you have any plans for lunch?"

"Remember when I told you I was going to try to get pregnant?"

JoBeth, who had just lifted her sandwich to take a bite, stopped. "Yes."

Rebecca smiled. "Well, it's happened. I'm almost four months along."

"Rebecca! And you didn't *tell* me!"

"I'm telling you now."

"But four months! I can't believe you've kept it secret all this time."

"I wanted to be sure there weren't going to be problems. Not that I was worried, but still... But anyway, now I've passed the first trimester and everything is going well...and the best part..." Her smile got bigger. "They told me it's a boy."

JoBeth still looked stunned. "I hardly know what to say."

"Oh, JoBeth, say you're happy for me, because I'm thrilled. You know how much I wanted this."

"Sweetie, if this is what you really want, of course I'm happy for you." Now JoBeth did take that bite, and for a long moment she chewed thoughtfully. "It is gonna be tough, though. You know that."

"I know, but it'll be worth it. I'll make whatever sacrifices I have to make to give my child the best possible life."

JoBeth nodded. "What about your family? Were they surprised?"

"I haven't told them yet." She started to say Jo-Beth was the first person she'd told, but that wasn't true, and Rebecca didn't want to tell any more lies than were absolutely necessary. "I'm going to call my mother tonight."

"How do you think she'll react?"

Rebecca shrugged. "I don't know. I hope she'll be glad for me. Eventually I'm sure she will, but at first I'm afraid this might be a shock."

"You never told her what you were thinking about doing?"

"No."

JoBeth frowned. "Why not? You two are so close."

Rebecca grimaced. "I was afraid she might try to talk me out of it."

JoBeth frowned. "Yeah, from what you've told me about your mother, she probably would have. You know, I'm curious. Do you have any idea of who the father...er, what's the politically correct term?"

"Donor," Rebecca said, chuckling.

"Okay, do you know who the *donor* might be? Do they tell you anything?"

"Oh, sure." Rebecca was prepared for this question. "They give you a complete profile on him."

"Really? Well, c'mon, tell me. What do you know about him?"

"Well, I know he's a professional in his late thirties and that he has brown hair and blue eyes. They also told me he's well educated." She had decided to fudge a bit on his age because she didn't want the profile to fit Kyle too closely, even though she didn't think anyone would ever make the connection.

"Wonder why he did it? Doesn't sound as if someone like that would need the money," JoBeth mused.

Rebecca shrugged. "I don't care why he did it. I'm just glad there are men who do."

JoBeth nodded. "What about the rest of the people in the office? When are you going to tell them? I mean, four months. I'm surprised you're not showing yet."

"Oh, I'm showing," Rebecca said, relieved that JoBeth hadn't continued questioning her about the baby's father. "I've just disguised it well. But my clothes are getting awfully tight. In fact, I'm going to start wearing maternity clothes next week."

"So you'll have to tell them."

"What I was hoping," Rebecca said slowly, "is that you'd kind of spread the news. I thought I'd tell Mark myself, this afternoon, and you could put the bug in Chloe's ear later today."

JoBeth chuckled. "That'll certainly do it. Everyone else will know before quitting time."

"Exactly."

They grinned at each other.

During their elevator ride back to the office, Jo-Beth said, "Listen, kiddo, I want you to know, you're not alone in this. I'll do anything I can to help."

Rebecca gave her a grateful smile. "I knew I could count on you."

"You planning to do the Lamaze thing?"

"Yes, I think so."

"Want me to be your partner?"

Rebecca grinned. "That would be great." Impulsively she hugged JoBeth. "Thanks."

"You're very welcome."

The elevator doors swished open, and the two women exited. Waving goodbye to JoBeth, Rebecca headed straight to Mark's office. No time like the present to get this over with.

"Is he busy?" she asked Chloe, who sat primping at her desk.

"I don't think so," Chloe said, capping her lipstick and putting it back into her makeup bag.

"Hey, come on in," Mark said when she knocked at his open door.

She did, shutting the door behind her. She hid a smile, knowing the closed door would pique Chloe's curiosity.

He gave her a quizzical look as she sat down. "Is something wrong?"

"Oh, no," Rebecca said. Now she did smile. "Just the opposite, in fact."

To Mark's credit, he betrayed no shock or disapproval as she told him her news. Not even when she explained that she'd been artificially inseminated. Not that Rebecca had expected him to say anything negative. First of all, even if he did disapprove, he was too much of a gentleman to say so. And secondly, Mark was one of the most nonjudgmental people she knew. His philosophy was, if it doesn't hurt anyone, it's your business what you believe or what you do. Still, she had felt a small twinge of anxiety over this first, public disclosure.

"Congratulations," he said, his dark eyes warm. "You'll make a wonderful mother."

"Thank you. And I want you to know this condition won't affect my work here."

"I never thought it would."

"I am going to need to take some time off, though, when the baby comes."

"No problem. We have a policy of giving a three-month paid pregnancy leave to our female employees."

"Even me?"

"Why not you?"

"Well, I thought, since I'm not married—"

"That isn't relevant."

She smiled gratefully, thinking what a really nice man he was. "Thank you, Mark."

"I'm a little envious, you know." His smile was rueful. "Brooke and I, well, we'd love to have kids, but it just hasn't happened yet."

Since Rebecca didn't know how to respond to this uncharacteristic confidence, she said only, "You two would make great parents."

He smiled and nodded, then briskly said, "I don't want you to worry about anything. You're a valued employee and we'll all help in any way we can."

Rebecca was still smiling an hour later when the Chloe network moved into high gear. Several co-workers popped their heads into Rebecca's door over the course of the early afternoon to congratulate her and "pump me for more information" as she laughingly told JoBeth later. Without exception, they were supportive, though. Rebecca was touched by their interest and genuine good wishes and their offers of help. How lucky she was, she told herself over and over again.

She tried not to think about Kyle, because when she thought about him, she only made herself unhappy. She couldn't afford that kind of negative thinking, especially not now, with the phone call to her mother looming.

That night, she waited until eight-thirty before calling home. Her mother answered on the second ring. "Hi, honey," she said. "I was just thinking about you."

"You were?"

"Yes. I was wondering what you'd like for your birthday."

"I'd forgotten all about my birthday." Rebecca's thirty-fifth birthday was coming up in a couple of weeks.

"Well, I didn't."

"You're supposed to remember. You're my mother. That's your job," Rebecca teased.

Her mother laughed, they talked for a while longer and Rebecca was finally persuaded to give her mother a list of possible options for a birthday present. Then, taking a deep breath, she said, "Listen, Mom, I, uh, have something to tell you."

"Oh?" Lucy Taylor's voice immediately sobered.

"Are you sitting down?"

"No. I'm standing here talking on the kitchen phone."

"Maybe you should sit down."

"Rebecca," her mother said, "you're scaring me. What is it? You're not ill, are you?"

Rebecca smiled. "Well, this does having something to do with my physical condition, but no, I'm not ill. In fact, I feel better than I've ever felt in my whole life."

"Well, what is it, then?"

"Mom . . . I'm pregnant."

Stunned silence followed. To Rebecca, the amount of time that passed seemed like an eternity before her mother said, "I—I didn't even know you were seeing anyone."

"I'm not."

"I don't understand."

This was going to be the hardest part. Rebecca had rarely told her mother a falsehood. She hated lying to her now, but she knew this was the best course—for her, for her unborn child and for her mother. "I was artificially inseminated."

"Oh, my . . ."

They talked for a long time after that. Lucy asked dozens of questions, expressed a dozen more concerns, and Rebecca tried to answer everything as well as assuage her mother's fears.

"Darling, you know that your family will support you one hundred percent," her mother said when their conversation had wound down.

"I know."

"Do you want me to tell your brothers?"

"Would you mind?"

"Of course not."

"And, Mom?"

"Yes, darling?"

"I—I was hoping you'd come and be with me when it's time... and afterward."

"Just try and keep me away."

Rebecca swallowed against the lump in her throat. "I love you," she said softly.

"I love you more," Lucy said.

After they'd hung up, Rebecca told herself again how lucky she was to have the kind of family and friends she had. Every time she started feeling sorry for herself because the man she loved didn't share her sentiments, she had better remind herself just how much she *did* have, which was tons more than so many women had.

That night she sorted through her clothes, and on Saturday she went shopping for some transitional outfits. She wanted some dresses that didn't look like maternity dresses, at least for the next couple of months.

The following Monday, she wore one of them to the office—a wine red tunic dress that was exceptionally complementary to her coloring. She took special care with her makeup and knew she looked better than she'd ever looked. A dozen people told her they agreed.

"Pregnancy agrees with you," said Sandra, a copywriter.

"Goodness, you look wonderful," said Marian, one of the graphic artists. She laughed. "Maybe I should try getting pregnant."

"Wow," said Dell, "what are you doing to yourself?" He made a mock leer. "Hey, babe, wanna meet me behind the water cooler?"

Even though she'd told herself she wasn't going to do this, Rebecca couldn't help wishing Kyle were there to see her. Her wayward thought angered her, because it told her she wasn't as resigned to her fate as she'd thought. *God, you're pathetic. Do you really think the sight of you in a maternity outfit is going to make him magically realize the error of his ways?*

For the rest of the day she kept her mind off her pregnancy and on her work. But at about four o'clock, Chloe approached her and said the office wanted to host a baby shower for her on Friday afternoon. "Mark said it's okay. We thought we'd start at four."

"But, Chloe, this *week?* I mean, I'm thrilled, but why not wait until it's closer to my due date?"

"We're excited. We don't want to wait. Besides, Candy's last day is Friday—" Candy was one of the graphic artists "—and she wants to be there, too. Come on, let us do this for you. What's the big deal? Now or later...same difference...and this way you'll have a good start on the things you need."

"Well, okay." Rebecca really *was* thrilled. She steadfastly refused to think about Kyle and the fact that there would be no father to pick her up afterward to load all the baby gifts into the car. Later that day, though, she had no choice but to think about him, because he called. Rebecca's heart beat faster at the sound of his voice.

"I've been out of town for a few days," he said. "That's why I haven't called you."

"Oh? A business trip?"

"Yes. I spent three days up in the Napa Valley at the Valeria Brothers winery. I think we have a good shot at getting their business."

"That's wonderful." Valeria Brothers was one of the largest wineries in the country.

"Yeah, they said one of the reasons they agreed to talk to me was because of the campaign the agency did for Hill Country Wines a few years back."

Rebecca smiled. The Hill Country campaign had been the one to put Alonzo & Christopher on the map.

They talked for a while longer about Kyle's visit to the winery, and all the time Rebecca was wondering if she should introduce the subject of the baby. She wanted to tell him she'd found out it was a boy, but she felt awkward unless he said something first.

A few seconds went by, and he said, "How, uh, have you been feeling?"

"Great. I feel great."

She was just about to say she'd had the ultrasound when he said, "That's good. Well, I guess I'd better get back to work. My desk is piled up with messages and mail," and her opportunity passed.

After they'd hung up, Rebecca wished she had just plunged in and told him. She even considered calling him back, but then she'd have to explain why she hadn't said anything to begin with. No, she didn't want to make a big deal out of not telling him. But she would remedy the situation the first chance she got. Kyle was bound to call her again in a few days, and she would definitely tell him then.

On Friday, Rebecca wore a new maternity outfit. It was sea-foam green and made out of some kind of blend that looked like silk crepe. The top was a long tunic with a rolled neckline and three-quarter sleeves, and it was paired with a short skirt that showed Rebecca's legs to advantage. It was very flattering, and made Rebecca feel feminine and pretty. Since the shower was a special occasion, she even wore her hair down, held away from her face with a black velvet band.

An air of excitement permeated the office that afternoon, and about three o'clock, Chloe and a couple other of the younger women stood on chairs and festooned the ceilings and walls of the conference room with blue balloons and blue crepe paper. A huge banner declared It's A Boy! The women had ordered a special cake in the shape of a baby carriage and Anna, the file clerk, had brought in several kinds of dips and chips.

At four o'clock, Rebecca, who had been told not to show her face until they were completely ready for her, was ceremoniously escorted to the party by JoBeth and Chloe.

"Here. Wear this hat," Chloe said, giggling. "I made it myself."

Rebecca laughed when she saw the concoction of rattles, blue flowers and white satin ribbons, but like a good sport, she allowed Chloe to put it on her head.

JoBeth aimed her camera. "Say cheese."

Again Rebecca laughingly obliged.

The next hour was filled with hilarity as Rebecca opened the presents that were piled on one end of the conference table and the surrounding floor. Several times she had to blink back tears at her co-workers' generosity. From Mark and Brooke, who hadn't been able to come because she was off covering a story in the southern part of the state, was a beautiful stroller. JoBeth gave her an infant car seat, and Chloe and the receptionist chipped in and bought Rebecca a baby monitor. From the others there were receiving blankets and gowns and bibs and toys. Dell and several of the other men had gone together to give her a gift certificate to a popular baby store.

"I don't know how to thank you," Rebecca said, overwhelmed as she looked at her loot.

After the presents were open, Chloe started serving the food. Rebecca was eating a piece of cake and listening to Dell tell a story, when a familiar voice said, "Hey, what's going on? Are we having a party?"

Her heart skipped a beat. She turned slowly.

A smiling Kyle, his eyes curious, stood in the doorway.

It took Kyle a few minutes to realize exactly what kind of a party it was. When he did, he felt as if someone had punched him. He struggled to compose himself as he walked into the conference room and returned everyone's greetings. Out of the corner of his eye, he read the banner It's A Boy! A boy? Rebecca knew it was a boy? Why hadn't she told him? When he'd talked to her the other day, she hadn't said a word about knowing the baby's sex.

A boy.

He swallowed. He was going to have a son.

"Hey, Kyle," someone said.

"We didn't know you were coming into town," someone else said.

"Surprised?" JoBeth said.

For one startled moment, Kyle thought he'd spoken his thoughts aloud.

"Or did Rebecca tell you she was pregnant?" JoBeth continued.

"She told me," he said stiffly, finally allowing himself to look at Rebecca. She looked incredibly pretty sitting there surrounded by baby gifts. Her eyes were shining and her cheeks were a becoming pink. Why hadn't she told him?

She smiled, and he could see she was trying very hard to act natural, even though her gaze only met his briefly before sliding away. "Just look at all these wonderful presents," she said brightly.

"I wish you guys had told me about this," he said to Chloe. "I would have gotten a present, too." He knew he sounded peevish, but he couldn't seem to help himself. He was still grappling with the news that he had fathered a son and that Rebecca had known about it for days and hadn't called him. She'd probably known about this shower for days, too, and she hadn't told him about it, either.

"The reason you weren't invited is I didn't know you were coming in to town today," Chloe said.

Chloe's reasoning did not placate him, yet he knew if he said anything further he would just be calling unwelcome attention to himself. He fought to get his emotions under control. Trouble was, he had been looking forward to seeing Rebecca and talking to her. He had planned to ask her to have dinner with him later tonight. He'd wanted to talk to her about his grandfather.

He couldn't understand why she hadn't told him. What was it? he thought resentfully. He was good enough to get her pregnant, but he wasn't good enough to be included in anything else?

"Here, Kyle," Anna said. "Have some cake." She held out a plate.

For the next thirty minutes or so, Kyle looked at the baby presents and made the appropriate remarks and talked to his co-workers and acted the way he always acted, but simmering under the surface was his mounting frustration and resentment. Now he really wanted to talk to Rebecca—and he wasn't in the mood to wait, either—but he couldn't figure out how to get her alone.

By six o'clock, people started drifting away. Chloe and Anna began cleaning up, and JoBeth started stacking Rebecca's presents.

Suddenly Kyle had an idea. He looked at Rebecca. "You can't take that stuff home by yourself."

"Oh, I know."

"Well," he said offhandedly, as if he'd just thought of it, "why don't you have dinner with me tonight, and we can take all that stuff in my car?"

"I'm sorry, Kyle, I can't. I'm having dinner with JoBeth."

"Yeah," JoBeth chimed in. "I picked her up this morning, so we're taking everything home in my car."

He shrugged. "All right. It was just a thought."

"You could always come with us," JoBeth said.

But Kyle had no interest in joining them. He was tired and irritated and he didn't want to have to pretend in front of a third party. "Thanks, but I really should go see my grandfather tonight, anyway." He avoided Rebecca's gaze. "You ready to take this stuff out to the car? I'll get some of the guys and we'll do it for you."

"That'd be great," JoBeth said.

He almost left without saying goodbye to Rebecca, but at the last minute sanity returned and he looked at her and smiled. "Have fun tonight."

"Thanks."

A few minutes later, loaded down with baby presents, he walked out to the garage with Dell and Mark and two of the other guys.

"Boy, you gotta hand it to Rebecca," Dell said. "She's one gutsy chick." He laughed and poked Kyle in the ribs. "One sexy chick, too. I wish she'd've told me she wanted a baby. She wouldn't have had to go get artificially inseminated. I would've been happy to do the honors."

The others laughed.

For one insane moment, Kyle was tempted to hit Dell. Instead, he gave him a scathing look and said, "Grow up." Then, jaw clenched, he stalked ahead.

Behind him, the other four men looked at each other in silent puzzlement.

Chapter Eleven

Rebecca had a hard time sleeping Friday night. She was mad at herself for the unexpected and completely avoidable ending to the baby shower.

You should have told Kyle about the shower when you talked to him on Wednesday. Then he wouldn't have been blindsided.

Remembering the look on his face when he had realized exactly what was happening in the conference room, she cringed. Although he'd recovered quickly, Rebecca knew him so well, she'd been acutely aware of his shock.

And his hurt.

And as much as she wished she could tell herself that he had no reason to be hurt, she knew that wasn't true. He had every reason. And uppermost among those reasons was the glaring fact that, of all their friends and co-workers, he was the last person to know the baby was going to be a boy.

Rebecca tried to put herself in his place. She could imagine what he'd been thinking and feeling. If it *had* been her, she would have felt completely betrayed.

And then, to top everything off, there was also his frustration over the evening. Rebecca knew, from his invitation to dinner, that he'd wanted to see her alone. There, however, she felt no cause for remorse. If he'd wanted to spend the evening with her, he should have called her before coming to Cleveland. The trouble was, Kyle took her for granted. Almost always, when he'd issued an invitation, she accepted. Even if she'd had tentative plans, she'd canceled them, because being with Kyle had always been the most important thing in her life.

But now there was something—*someone*—more important. Her baby. And directly affecting her baby was her own emotional well-being.

So even if she could have canceled her plans to be with JoBeth that evening—which she couldn't—she wouldn't have.

She felt too vulnerable right now. Being with Kyle, hiding her true feelings, was becoming harder and harder. She was afraid that one of these days she might give herself away. And then what?

On and on her thoughts went. Finally, long after midnight, she fell asleep. Consequently, she slept later than usual for a Saturday morning. So she was just having her first cup of coffee at nine-thirty when the doorbell rang.

Sighing, thinking it was probably one of the children from the neighborhood selling raffle tickets or something similar, Rebecca walked to the front door.

Her heart tripped when she saw Kyle standing on the front porch.

"Kyle! Wh-what are you doing here?"

He tried, but his smile just missed the mark. "Would you believe I was in the neighborhood?"

Rebecca's startled eyes took in his casual jeans-clad appearance, the blue shirt that matched his eyes and the way the sun glinted off his freshly-cut hair, even as her mind whirled with unspoken questions.

She was acutely aware of her own state of undress and how vulnerable it made her feel. "Come on in," she said as she fought to get her reeling emotions under control. "I was just having my first cup of coffee. Would you like some?"

"Sure." With a disturbing reminder of the time they'd shared under this roof, he walked into the kitchen and unerringly opened the cupboard where she stored her mugs. While he poured himself coffee, Rebecca tightened the belt of her cotton robe and told herself to calm down. She fervently wished she were dressed and had her makeup on.

"Did you have a good time last night?" he asked once they were settled at the dining room table.

"Yes." She was very glad she'd put all the baby presents into the second bedroom—the one she planned to use as the nursery. There was no sense in rubbing salt into the wound.

"Where'd you go?" He took a drink of his coffee, his blue eyes meeting hers over the rim of the cup.

Rebecca hid her nervousness behind her own cup. "We went to a Japanese restaurant out in Solon that JoBeth has been telling me about, and it was great." B.B. or Before Baby, Rebecca might have suggested that she and Kyle try it for their next dinner out, but those days were long gone. "How was your evening? Is your grandfather doing okay now?"

He shrugged. "I don't know. I'm worried about him. He seems frail and much weaker than he did before."

"I'm sorry."

"Yeah," he said, his expression darkening. "I really hate leaving him again." He stared down into his cup. "I'm not sure I'm doing the right thing taking this job in L.A."

Rebecca's heart slammed in her chest as the import of his words sank in. Oh, God, what would she do if he decided not to go back to L.A.? She couldn't handle it. She couldn't! As her thoughts raced, silence fell between them. Rebecca frantically searched for something else—anything else—to say, as if changing the subject would somehow erase the problem. Just as she was beginning to feel desperate for another topic of conversation, he spoke.

"Why didn't you tell me the baby is a boy?"

She swallowed. Here it was. The reason for his visit. "I—I guess I didn't think of it."

"You didn't *think* of it?"

Rebecca stared at him. It didn't take a genius to see he was furious. Suddenly, all of her compassion for him, all of her empathy, disappeared, and a corresponding anger flooded her. "That's not quite true," she said defiantly. "I *did* think of it. But frankly, I wasn't sure you cared."

He set his mug down with a thump and coffee splashed onto the tablecloth. They both ignored it. His eyes had turned to blue ice. "That's a helluva thing to say."

"Well, I'm sorry, but it's true." And it was true. And maybe, in some subconscious realm she had not been aware of, she had been subtly punishing him for not asking more questions about their child. For not... *For not loving me....*

"Just what have I ever done or said to make you think I didn't care?" he demanded.

As suddenly as it had flared, Rebecca's anger died away. He had a right to be angry. She didn't. She sighed wearily. "Oh, God, I'm sorry, Kyle. I—" She broke off in consternation. This was impossible. How could she explain? Why didn't he just go away and leave her alone?

"I *am* the baby's father," he said. "So of course I care. And even if I wasn't the father, I'm your friend, Rebecca. Your *best* friend. Or at least I thought I was. But maybe that's all changed now?"

Rebecca looked away. She was dangerously close to tears. There was so much she couldn't say, so much she couldn't allow herself to feel. She told herself to be strong. When she finally faced him again, she had managed to get herself under control. "Look, Kyle," she said slowly and calmly, "this whole situation is very awkward for me, just as I'm sure it is for you. I knew it would be. That's why I never suggested it until I found out you were leaving Cleveland. I mean, seriously, how can we continue to have the same kind of relationship we had before? Everything *has* changed. And—'' she took a deep breath ''—we *did* agree that once I became pregnant, you would no longer be involved. I think it's best we stick to that agreement.''

''So what are you saying? That you're not interested in continuing our friendship at all? That you want me to disappear from your life completely?''

''No, of course not. I just...'' She closed her eyes. ''I don't know what I want.''

He stood abruptly. ''I knew this would turn out to be a mistake. I wish I'd never agreed to do it.''

Rebecca stared at him helplessly. She would have given anything to start this conversation over and do it differently. Somehow she had mishandled the situation badly.

While she was still trying to think of what she could say to smooth things over, he muttered a tight ''I've got to get going. My grandfather's expecting me.'' His eyes were cold. ''Sorry I bothered you. I won't do it again.''

After spending the afternoon and evening with his grandfather, Kyle had simmered down and was even beginning to feel a bit ashamed of his outburst at Rebecca's.

She was right. The situation *was* awkward. And maybe she should have told him about the baby's sex and the shower, but was it really *that* big of a deal that she hadn't?

You acted like an ass this morning.

Ruefully, he decided he'd better call her tomorrow and apologize.

He left his grandfather's before ten because the old man was obviously tired. But Kyle wasn't. He felt wired and had no desire to go home to his empty condo. He decided he would pay a visit to the night basketball league instead, even though he'd said his goodbyes weeks ago.

It took him about thirty minutes to get to St. Rosco's Church, which was downtown near Ohio City. As expected, the gymnasium was lighted and several cars and bikes and motorbikes were parked in the parking lot next to it.

The dozen or so boys and the three older men who were coaching and supervising waved and called out to Kyle as he entered the gym. Kyle greeted them, happy to see that Enos Madison was one of them.

Kyle sat down and watched the game in progress. Enos was playing at the power forward position tonight, and after a dazzling three-pointer, which won the game for his team, he headed in Kyle's direction. There would be a thirty-minute rest period, then another game would start at midnight. Most of the boys would stay on, Kyle knew, and play until the gym closed at two o'clock. Enos was usually one of them.

"Hey, Kyle, thought you was gone," Enos said, grinning widely and dropping down onto the bench next to Kyle. He was still mopping sweat from his face and neck. "Good to see you, man." He held up his hand, and they high-fived.

"I came in for the weekend, so thought I'd stop by and see how you guys are doing."

Enos shrugged. "We doin' okay."

Something about the youngster's voice caused Kyle to look at him more closely. "You sure? You sound like something's wrong. Is it your father?" Enos's father periodically skipped out on his family, leaving his wife to cope with supporting their five children. But Able Madison had come home before Christmas and had landed a good job as a security guard with a new apartment complex. Kyle hadn't told Enos, but he'd worked quietly behind the scenes to help Able get the job, which included a rent-free apartment. Seeing the family move into someplace safer and more secure than their previous living quarters had been all the thanks Kyle needed.

"Nah. Pop, he's okay. He's doin' good, as a matter of fact," Enos said.

"Something's wrong, though," Kyle pressed.

Enos shrugged again, his strong, young shoulders looking oddly defenseless.

"Tell you what," Kyle said, "why don't we go get a burger somewhere?"

Enos nodded, and after saying their goodbyes, the two of them walked out to the parking lot. "How'd you get here tonight?" Kyle said.

"Rode with Robert."

Kyle drove to a nearby Burger King. He waited until they were settled with their food in front of them before saying, "Okay, what is it?"

Enos's dark eyes were troubled as they met Kyle's across the table. "I got this girlfriend, you know...."

Kyle smiled. "Lisha." He'd met the pretty sophomore one night when she'd tagged along with Enos. "What's the problem? Did she break up with you?"

Enos shook his head, then looked down at his chocolate milkshake. "Nah. Nuthin like that. She—she's pregnant, man."

Kyle put his sandwich down. "Oh."

Enos just sat there, staring at his food.

"The baby's yours?" Kyle asked.

"I guess so," Enos said.

"What do you mean, you guess so? Do you have any reason to think Lisha is seeing anyone else?" *Damn.* Kyle couldn't help but feel sorry for the kid. After all, he was only sixteen. And Lisha might not even be that old.

"She wasn't seein' anyone else," Enos mumbled.

"What are you going to do? Have you told your parents? Has she told hers?"

Enos finally looked up. "Me? I ain't gonna do nuthin. I told her she's on her own. I don't wanna be no father." His voice had taken on an edge of desperation.

Kyle was about to say something like, "Well, then you should have kept your pants zipped up," but he stopped just in time. Lectures would do no good. What's done was done. Now he needed to help Enos find some answers. "What did Lisha say when you said that?"

Enos looked away. "She . . . she cried."

Kyle waited.

"Anybody woulda done the same thing," Enos finally said. "Wouldn't they?"

Kyle could see the boy was confused and frightened. He could also see that Enos wasn't nearly as uncaring and unfeeling as his harsh words to Lisha might have made him seem. "Look, Enos," he said, picking his words carefully, "I understand how scared you are, but one of the things a man has to do if he ever wants to be considered a man is take responsibility for his actions.

"Lisha didn't get pregnant by herself," Kyle continued. "So whether or not you want to be a father is not the important consideration. The fact is, you're *going* to be a father. Your only choice is whether you'll be a good one or a bad one."

Enos stared at him.

"The first step to being a good father would be for you to tell your parents what's happened."

"Oh, man," Enos said, his face twisting, "my dad's gonna kill me."

"Your father isn't going to kill you. In fact, you can tell your father to call me. Here..." Kyle dug out his wallet. "Here's my number in California. I'm going back tomorrow. He can call me there, anytime, collect. Okay?"

"O-okay." He swallowed, his Adam's apple bobbing. When he met Kyle's gaze again, his dark eyes were still troubled, but much of the panic Kyle had seen earlier was gone. "I—I don't know nuthin about bein' a father."

"Nobody does until it happens."

Long after he'd taken Enos home, first wringing a promise from the boy that he'd talk to his parents the following day, Kyle thought about Enos's situation and compared it to his own. His words to the boy haunted him. *A man has to take responsibility for his actions... It doesn't matter whether you wanted to be a father or not. Your only choice is whether you'll be a good father or a bad father....*

Kyle told himself that his situation with Rebecca was nothing like Enos's with Lisha. Lisha wanted and needed Enos's help and involvement in raising their child. Rebecca did not.

As the first blush of dawn tinted the horizon, Kyle got up and made a pot of coffee. He took a mugful out to his small balcony and stood at the rail watching the sunrise as he drank it.

For the first time since finding out about Rebecca's pregnancy, he asked himself what, exactly, he wanted. He wasn't entirely sure, but he did know one thing. He no longer wanted to live in Los Angeles. And maybe, subconsciously, he had not wanted this for a long time. Otherwise, why hadn't he given up his riverfront condo? He'd told himself that he'd need a place to stay as long as his grandfather was alive and he would be visiting Cleveland often, but that wasn't true. He could easily have stayed at his grandfather's.

He also admitted that even though he wouldn't be able to participate in his child's life, he wanted the chance to at least observe it from the sidelines.

It was ironic, he finally concluded.

His life had been so carefully thought out.

He'd known exactly what he'd wanted and what he hadn't wanted. And now, through a twist of fate, he'd discovered that maybe he didn't know himself nearly as well as he'd thought he did. Unfortunately, this discovery had come too late, he thought wearily. He'd made his deal with Rebecca. She'd been living up to her end of their bargain.

So he would have to continue to live up to his.

Whether he wanted to or not.

Before leaving for the airport, Kyle called Rebecca and apologized for his behavior of the day before.

"It's okay," she said. "I understand. It's awkward for both of us, isn't it?"

He conceded that it was and terminated the conversation shortly thereafter. He didn't feel comfortable talking to her right now. He knew he had to sort out his feelings first and figure out what he was going to do about them. So even though he had determined he didn't want to go back to L.A. on a permanent basis, he was actually glad to go back for now.

The first two days after he returned, he was too busy to spend much time thinking. Then, on Wednesday, two things happened. That morning, Kyle realized it was Rebecca's birthday and he called and ordered flowers, paying a small fortune to ensure their delivery to the office that afternoon. And at four o'clock, a distraught Hugo called.

"Kyle, your grandfather has had a heart attack."

Kyle closed his eyes. "Is—is he . . . ?" He couldn't finish the question.

"He's stabilized for now. I'm calling from the hospital."

"Which one? University?"

"Yes. He's in the coronary care unit."

"What does his doctor say about his chances?"

"They really don't know. The first twenty-four hours are the crucial ones. And..." Hugo's voice broke. "He's eighty-six."

"I'll get on the next flight out. Give me a number where I can call you back."

After booking his flight, Kyle called Mark at home and explained the situation. "I'm really sorry to leave you in the lurch like this, with the office barely open and so many things hanging fire."

"Look, don't worry about it," Mark said. "Just do what you have to do. If necessary, Simon or I or Jim Browning from the New York office will come out there and take charge until you can get back."

Kyle thanked Mark, then called Rebecca. She wasn't there. Of course not, he thought distractedly. It was her birthday. She was probably out somewhere, celebrating. He left a message on her answering machine, then headed for the Santa Monica apartment he'd rented only weeks earlier.

On the way he prayed his grandfather would make it.

Rebecca spent her birthday with JoBeth. They went to a movie and out for a pizza afterward.

"Not a very exciting way to spend a birthday," JoBeth said.

"Being with a good friend is a *perfect* way to spend a birthday," Rebecca assured her. But she couldn't help remembering last year's birthday. Kyle had taken her to Severance Hall to hear the Cleveland Symphony Orchestra play, and afterward they'd had dinner at one of the most elegant restaurants in the city.

His birthday present had been wonderful, too—an exquisitely detailed antique gold bracelet that had made Rebecca gasp with delight.

"Yeah, well, personally, if it were my birthday, I'd like to have a sugar daddy who'd fly me to Paris and take me to Maxim's," JoBeth said glumly.

Rebecca laughed. "You? You want a sugar daddy? I thought you'd sworn off men."

"That was last week."

"What happened to 'who needs 'em?'" Rebecca teased, mimicking JoBeth's oft-spouted phrase.

JoBeth grinned. "Aw, hell, you're right. Who needs 'em? We're doing just fine without men in our lives, aren't we?" She reached down on the seat beside her, handing Rebecca a gaily wrapped package. "Here. Happy Birthday."

Rebecca smiled when she opened the package and found her favorite strawberry bath gel and a loofah sponge to go with it. She tried not to think about JoBeth's casually tossed-off comment concerning men. How Rebecca wished she was doing just fine without a man in her life. How much easier it would be if she could make herself stop missing Kyle, if she could make herself stop wishing things were different. Lord knows, she'd tried to forget about him, but something always happened to sabotage her efforts.

Like today, for instance. She'd been going along just fine, accepting birthday congratulations from her co-workers, talking to her mother and brothers—all of whom called throughout the course of the day—enjoying the cake and ice cream that was a tradition in the office. And then the flowers had arrived.

Tiny pink roses. Her favorite flower. Dozens of them.

They were so beautiful.

She hadn't had to open the card to know who'd sent them. Her eyes misted as she read Kyle's message "Have a wonderful birthday. Love, Kyle."

The *love* meant nothing, she knew, but even so, her heart ached as she looked at the word. Kyle always signed his cards and gifts this way. To him, the word *love* just meant he cared, the way he'd care for any good friend or family member.

She buried her face in the fragrant blossoms and tried not to cry.

How, she wondered now, as she and JoBeth finished their pizza, was she ever going to get to the point where she could say what JoBeth had said and mean it?

Kyle took the red-eye to Cleveland, arriving at six the next morning. He went straight to the hospital. Hugo was sitting in the waiting area outside Coronary Care, and he seemed pathetically happy to see Kyle. Kyle's heart ached for the older man. He looked around. "Where's Dad? And Kevin?"

"Your father *was* here," Hugo said, "but he left a couple of hours ago." At Kyle's thunderous look, Hugo added quickly, "He's coming back. He said to tell you he'd see you later."

"And Kevin?" Kyle said.

"Kevin's in the Bahamas. I couldn't reach him. Your father said he'd try again this morning. No one seemed to know what hotel he was staying at."

Kyle grimaced. Since his brother's divorce, he'd been living the high life, and each female companion living it with him seemed to get younger and younger. "So how's Gramps? Can I see him?"

"He seems to be responding well. The doctors are encouraged."

"Thank God."

Hugo pointed to the double doors leading to the coronary care unit. "Go in there and tell the nurse who you are. She'll take you to his room. They only allow two people in during any hour period, and then for only ten minutes."

"You coming with me?"

"No. You go on. He'll want to see you alone first."

Kyle nodded and entered the CCU. An older nurse with sympathetic dark eyes told him to go to Unit 8. "Down the hall, last door on your right. And, Mr. MacNeill?"

"Yes?"

"He's hooked up to all kinds of machines. That's normal. Don't be alarmed."

Even though the nurse had warned him, Kyle wasn't completely prepared for the sight that greeted him when he entered his grandfather's room. His heart gave a painful wrench as he saw how frail and old Graham MacNeill looked. His eyes were closed, an IV was attached by tube to his left hand and the surrounding machines pulsed and beat and beeped around him, giving a surreal feeling to the atmosphere. The smells of age and antiseptic and medicine and sickness permeated the air.

"Gramps?" he whispered.

His grandfather's eyes opened. At first he blinked, and then, recognizing Kyle, he smiled. "Kyle." His voice was thready.

A rush of love brought a sting to Kyle's eyes. He walked closer to the bed and took his grandfather's free hand. For a moment, neither spoke.

Then his grandfather said weakly, "Glad . . . to see you."

Kyle nodded, overcome by emotion. "I'm glad to see you, too. You scared the liver out of us."

Graham attempted another smile. "Guess...you're stuck with me for a while longer."

Kyle chuckled, grateful his grandfather felt well enough to joke. "I guess we are."

Graham's eyes closed briefly, but he squeezed Kyle's hand, and Kyle returned the pressure. A long moment passed. Just as Kyle was sure his grandfather had fallen asleep again, Graham opened his eyes and looked at him. "I'm not afraid to die," he said clearly and with more strength than he'd exhibited since Kyle had arrived.

"Well, that's good, but you don't have to worry—"

"I only have one regret." His blue gaze fastened intently to Kyle's. "That I probably won't live long enough to see you marry."

"Gramps..."

"I just want you to be happy. And . . . it sure would be nice to have a great-grandchild to carry on the MacNeill name...."

Kyle almost smiled. His grandfather certainly knew the right buttons to push. But he didn't smile, because he suddenly felt too guilty to do so.

"Oh, it's all right. Don't worry about me," his grandfather continued softly. "I'm...just an old man...wishing for the impossible. I know it's not going to happen."

Chapter Twelve

Rebecca set her alarm for five-thirty Thursday morning. She'd decided last night, after getting Kyle's message, that she would drive to work this morning, stopping at University Hospital on the way.

She got to the hospital at seven-thirty and found Kyle in the waiting room outside Coronary Care. Two older men were with him. She recognized Hugo, his grandfather's companion, and figured the other man must be Kyle's father.

"Rebecca," Kyle said, eyes lighting as he rose to meet her.

Her heart contracted as she saw the worry lines around his mouth and eyes, the stubble covering his cheeks. "I got your message last night. I'm so sorry."

He kissed her cheek and hugged her briefly. "Thanks for coming."

The two older men had risen. Kyle turned, drawing her forward. "Dad, this is Rebecca Taylor, a good friend of mine. Hugo, you remember Rebecca, don't you?"

Rebecca shook hands with Hugo first, then turned to Kyle's father. She could see the resemblance between father and son in Donald MacNeill's square jaw with the hint of dimples and his warm smile. "You're the young woman who dragged Kyle out of that fire," he said.

"Well, I didn't really drag him."

"You saved his life, though."

Rebecca never knew what to say when anyone brought up the episode, so she took refuge in a noncommittal smile and shrug. Then, turning to Kyle, she said, "How's your grandfather doing?"

Kyle shrugged. "We don't know, but we hope he's going to pull through this. They tell us that if his condition is still stabilized by tonight, he should be out of the woods."

"I'll keep my fingers crossed."

"Miss Taylor," Hugo said with a courtly smile, "we were just about to go and have some breakfast. Would you like to join us?"

"Thank you, but I can't stay," Rebecca said. "I only stopped by for a minute. I'm on my way to work." She smiled. "It was nice to see you again." Turning to Donald MacNeill, she added, "And very nice to meet you, Mr. MacNeill."

"I'll walk you out to the parking lot," Kyle said, taking her arm.

"Oh, that's okay. You go ahead to breakfast."

"I need some fresh air." He looked at the two older men. "I'll meet you in the cafeteria."

After they were out of earshot, Kyle said, "It means a lot to me that you came today."

"Kyle... of course I came.... We're friends." *And I love you. What hurts you, hurts me.*

He nodded slowly. "Yes, but our friendship has been under a strain lately."

Rebecca sighed. "I know."

"Rebecca..." He put his hand on her arm, stopping her.

She looked up. Their eyes met.

"I don't want to lose your friendship. You're too important to me."

Rebecca's eyes filled with tears, and she had to look away. "You're important to me, too," she whispered.

"When everything's settled down... with my grandfather and all... I think we need to talk."

"All right." She had herself under control now and managed a smile.

They didn't speak again until they were outside in the bright May morning. Rebecca started to say goodbye, then, realizing she'd never thanked Kyle for the flowers, said instead, "I loved the pink roses. Thank you for remembering."

"You're welcome."

"And I'm so glad your grandfather seems to be doing well."

He nodded. "For how long, though? Hell, he's an old man. He's not going to live forever." His eyes were bleak.

More than anything, Rebecca wanted to put her arms around Kyle. To tell him she loved him.

"I just wish I hadn't let him down so often."

"Kyle, that's crazy. When have you let him down?"

"Lots of times. I didn't go into the business the way he wanted me to. I couldn't even save the chain from being sold to Consolidated. And I've disappointed him in other ways, too—" He broke off suddenly, shaking his head.

"In what ways?" Rebecca said, frowning.

"It's nothing. Don't pay any attention to me. I haven't had any sleep, so I'm not making a lot of sense." He squeezed her hand. "Thanks for coming. I'll call you later and let you know how things are going."

Long after she'd left him, Rebecca wondered what it was he'd started to say.

The following day, the heart specialist told Kyle, his father and Hugo that Graham was, indeed, doing much better. "We're going to move him into a private room this afternoon," the doctor said. "And in a few days, if he continues to improve and respond to the medication, we'll let him go home." Then he cautioned, "But he's going to need close attention." He shrugged. "After all, he's eighty-six. He could have another attack tomorrow, and the next time it could be fatal."

And the next time it could be fatal....

The doctor's warning pulsed in Kyle's brain for the rest of the day.

And the next time it could be fatal....

By the time Kyle left the hospital, he had made a decision.

That night he slept at his condo, because the nurses had assured him his grandfather would sleep through the night, and Kyle did not need to be there.

Early Friday morning he got up, showered, shaved, dressed in slacks and a knit shirt and loafers and walked the few short blocks to the office.

He headed straight for Mark's office. It was only seven forty-five, but Mark usually got in early. Sure enough, he was already sitting at his desk. Kyle walked in, shutting the door behind him.

"How's your grandfather?" Mark asked.

Kyle explained the situation. Then he said, "I'm sorry, Mark, but this episode has made me think about a lot of things, including my priorities. I know I'm letting you down, but it can't be helped." He met Mark's eyes squarely. "I've decided I don't want the L.A. job."

Mark looked at him for a long moment. Then, slowly, a wide smile spread across his face.

Kyle didn't know what kind of reaction he'd expected, but it certainly wasn't this.

"You can't imagine what a load you've taken off my mind," Mark said.

"I don't understand."

"Two days ago—only hours before you called me to tell me about your grandfather's attack, in fact—Brooke was offered the evening anchor spot at the NBC affiliate station in Los Angeles. She flew out there yesterday to accept the job."

As the import of Mark's words sank in, Kyle smiled, too. "I'm assuming that means you're moving to L.A. with Brooke?"

"I'm sure as hell not letting her go alone."

"So if you're going to L.A.," Kyle said, thinking aloud, "then the logical thing is for you to take over the L.A. office."

Mark nodded.

"And you weren't sure how to tell me."

"No, I wasn't. Simon and I talked it over yesterday, after I knew about your grandfather, and we decided we'd just wait and see how things went. But we did toss around some possibilities." Mark leaned back in his chair and rotated his pen between his fingers. "For instance, if you really wanted to stay in L.A., you could be the Director of Sales. What we'd hoped, of course, is that you'd agree to stay here and manage this office instead."

Kyle couldn't help grinning.

He refused to think about how Rebecca would react when she found out he wasn't leaving Cleveland after all. He also refused to think about how convenient it was for him that he now had an legitimate and unarguable excuse to do what he wanted to do anyway.

When Rebecca walked into the conference room for the three o'clock staff meeting, she was totally unprepared for the news that awaited her.

"Before we start going over accounts," Mark said, "I've got an announcement to make. I was going to wait until Kyle could be here, but I'm not sure when he'll be back in the office.'' By now everyone knew about Kyle's grandfather's heart attack.

Rebecca and JoBeth exchanged a what's-going-on-do-you-know? glance.

"A couple of days ago, Brooke was offered the anchor spot at the NBC affiliate station in Los Angeles,'' Mark continued.

"Wow, that's great,'' someone said, and others murmured their agreement.

"Needless to say,'' he went on, "I do not want a long-distance marriage.''

Everyone but Rebecca laughed.

"Consequently,'' Mark said, "I plan to join her in L.A. no later than mid-July.'' He paused, looked around. "This development has, of course, caused a few problems. But Kyle and I talked this morning and reached a mutually agreeable decision.''

Rebecca's stomach felt queasy.

"Naturally, if I'm going to be in L.A., the logical thing is for me to manage the L.A. office. Kyle agreed. So...'' Mark paused dramatically. "Starting July 1, Kyle will be managing this office instead.''

Rebecca sat there, stunned. She couldn't believe it. Kyle was not going to L.A. He would be there, in the Cleveland office, from now on.

Every day she would have to see him.

Every day she would have to go through the torture of pretending that all was well, that she was happy, that she and Kyle were no more than they'd ever been—friends and co-workers.

Every day she would have to maintain the fiction that she had been artificially inseminated and that Kyle had no relationship to her pregnancy.

How could she endure it?

How could she keep up such a pretense, day after day after day, especially after their child was born?

She couldn't.

She wouldn't.

Rebecca said nothing about the changes Mark had announced when she talked to Kyle that evening. She listened to his report on his grandfather, reassured him that all would be well and waited to see if he would say anything about the new development regarding his transfer to Los Angeles.

He didn't.

She didn't hear from him on Saturday, but she hadn't really expected to.

On Sunday afternoon he called to tell her his grandfather was going home. Once again he made no mention of his changed job status.

Rebecca was glad of the reprieve. She really didn't want to talk about Kyle not moving to L.A. until she'd figured out what she was going to do.

Sunday night she considered everything. Asked herself if she was being too melodramatic. Maybe she *could* manage to be in Kyle's orbit on a daily basis. But she quickly discarded that possibility. No. She'd settled that issue long ago. She couldn't manage. She would crack under the pressure. And an always-on-the-edge, always-afraid mother would not be good for her child.

So where did that leave her?

If Kyle wasn't going to Los Angeles, and she could not handle his presence in Cleveland, then she would have to be the one to leave.

There was no other way.

Kyle's father finally located Kevin MacNeill on Sunday. He refused to come home.

"What's the point of ruining my trip?" he said to Kyle. "The old man's okay now, and I was planning to come home on Wednesday anyway."

"That's a damned selfish attitude," Kyle said angrily.

"You're a fine one to talk," Kevin retorted.

"What's that supposed to mean?"

"You've been doing what you please for so long, you've forgotten some of us haven't. Hell, I've been toeing the line for years. Jumping to Dad's and the old man's demands, and frankly, I've had a bellyful. Besides, the old man doesn't care if I'm there. You're the fair-haired boy. We all know that."

Furious, Kyle said a tight-lipped goodbye and hung up. But his brother's taunt lingered. For years, Kyle had denied what he knew in his heart to be true. His grandfather *did* favor him. He'd always favored him. And his favoritism had hurt Kevin, who had covered up that hurt when he was younger by acting as if he didn't care and by avoiding contact with their grandfather as he became older.

It had been wrong of Graham MacNeill to show his favoritism, but the old man was only human. He'd made mistakes the same as everybody else. The same as Kyle.

Kyle thought about the monumental mistake he'd made only months ago. He knew now he should never have agreed to Rebecca's scheme. But how was he to know he would feel this way about her pregnancy?

About her. How you'd feel about her...

Now where had that thought come from?

He examined it. Were his feelings for Rebecca different now than they were before she'd gotten pregnant?

You know they are. You're in love with her. Why don't you admit it?

The realization staggered him.

He was in love with Rebecca, and there wasn't one damned thing he could do about it.

Rebecca went to work Monday morning, determined to talk to Kyle the moment he returned to the office. She didn't have long to wait. At nine o'clock he knocked on her door. "You busy?" he said.

"Yes, but come on in anyway. I was hoping we'd have a chance to talk today."

He walked in but he didn't sit. "Can it wait until tonight? That's why I stopped by, to see if you'd like to have a quick dinner with me after work and before I head to the hospital. Unless you have plans, of course...."

"No, no plans." She was relieved. She hadn't relished talking to him in her office where anyone might overhear.

"Five-thirty okay?"

"Fine."

For the remainder of the day, Rebecca stayed in her office. She even ate lunch at her desk. She just wasn't in the mood to talk to anyone, and she figured they were all buzzing about Kyle taking Mark's place and wondering whether there'd be any changes made. She also knew there were people who were jealous of Kyle, so she was sure there would be some snide remarks along with the speculation. She wasn't up to it. Pretending was too hard. It had been bad enough Friday afternoon when Mark made his announcement.

A few minutes after five-thirty, Kyle appeared in her doorway. "Ready?"

"Yes." Rebecca gathered her things, and they walked out together.

"How do you feel about Chinese?"

"I don't care. Whatever you want is fine with me."

"Let's eat at Hunan Kitchen then," he suggested, naming a restaurant only a couple of blocks from the office.

Rebecca decided she would wait until they'd reached the restaurant and ordered before bringing up the subject that had not been out of her mind since Friday.

Kyle beat her to it. Their waiter had no sooner left with their orders when he said, "I know you've heard the news."

"Yes. Mark announced it at the staff meeting Friday afternoon."

"What do you think?"

Rebecca met his gaze squarely. "If this is what you want, I'm glad for you."

"But what about you? How do you feel about it?"

Rebecca had rehearsed exactly what she'd say. "It won't work, Kyle. I think you know that. As far as I'm concerned, if you're going to be in Cleveland permanently, then I must leave."

"But why? Why won't it work if no one knows?"

She shrugged. "Trust me. It just won't." *Not unless you've suddenly realized you're in love with me. Not unless you want to marry me.* She knew it was stupid, but there was still a tiny flicker of hope burning somewhere deep inside.

The seconds ticked away. Rebecca picked up her water glass and took a drink. She waited for Kyle to say something. *If you'd only say you love me....*

"Look," he finally said, "let's leave that issue for now and talk about something else. I've been doing a lot of serious thinking lately. When someone close to you almost dies, you start to really think about what's important and what isn't. Anyway, I know what we agreed...about the baby. But I think it's only right for me to assume some of the responsibility for him. To have a part in his life."

"No!" She shook her head vehemently. *No, no, no.* If he didn't love her, if he didn't want to marry her, she had to cut all ties with Kyle. "No," she said more quietly, trying to calm her pounding heart. "We made a deal. This child is my responsibility. I don't want or need your help in raising him."

He stared at her. "I see."

Rebecca knew she'd hurt him. Oh, God, she'd been such a fool to think their friendship would ever survive this.

"Kyle, please, I don't want you to think I don't appreciate your offer. I know you're trying to do the right thing, and...and I admire you for it. But I really think it's better if we stick to our original agreement."

"You're calling the shots," he said stiffly. "So if that's what you want, that's what we'll do."

"But don't you agree that a clean break is best?" *Say no. Say you want me to stay. Say you want us to be a family. Say you love me....* "That way we can both get on with our lives."

"Yes, of course. You're absolutely right," he agreed. "I don't know what I was thinking. So when will you leave?"

With his words, the last glimmer of hope died away. Rebecca's heart felt as heavy as a stone when she answered. "As soon as I can." *The sooner, the better...*

The next hour was the longest and most difficult sixty minutes Rebecca had ever spent. She and Kyle ate. They even talked. But they avoided each other's eyes.

Rebecca wouldn't allow herself to think about what had just been decided. She forced her mind to concentrate on the food, on the people in the restaurant, on anything but the fact that soon everything in her life would change again and that Kyle would be lost to her forever.

Kyle knew there was nothing else he could have done but agree with Rebecca. He had tested the waters, and her nearly violent reaction had given him his answer.

She did not want him around.

This knowledge hurt. It hurt a lot.

Hey, you gambled, and you lost. Deal with it.

Despite everything she'd said when they'd made their agreement about the baby, he guessed he'd hoped that maybe...just maybe...she had some feelings for him.

Obviously she didn't.

Not the kinds of feelings he wanted her to have. For a moment there, he'd considered telling her the whole truth. *"I love you and I want to marry you. I want us to be a family and raise our child together."*

But how could he?

She'd made her feelings abundantly clear. It would have been unfair to put her on the spot that way. And she was right. They'd made a deal. She'd been upfront with him from the beginning, making it clear she wanted a baby from him and nothing more. Just because he'd had second thoughts didn't mean he had any right to try to force her to do something she didn't want to do.

For the remainder of their dinner, he was careful to act as if her rejection didn't matter. But it was a strain, and he couldn't wait to be alone. Finally it was time to leave and drive her to her car and go on to the hospital.

When they reached Van Aken Boulevard, he stopped the BMW behind her car and walked around to help her out. He had decided that he would shake her hand and say goodbye, then later tonight he would call Mark and tell him he was going to spend the rest of his time in Cleveland with his grandfather. Once his grandfather was settled at home and Kyle felt good about leaving him, he would head back to Los Angeles to get the ball rolling there for a smooth transition. That way, he could avoid having to see Rebecca again.

And by the time he finally returned to Cleveland, she would be long gone.

But at the last moment, just before she got into her car, Kyle simply couldn't end things that way. There was too much between them.

So when she raised her eyes to say goodbye, he leaned over and brushed her smooth cheek lightly with his lips. The delicate fragrance that always clung to her swept through him, leaving a trail of aching loneliness that he knew would not go away for a long time...if ever.

He put his arms around her and held her close for a moment. "What I told you before still goes," he said. "If ever you need anything or want anything, all you have to do is ask."

Chapter Thirteen

Kyle lay awake most of the night. The situation was more than ironic, he finally decided. And in some ways he deserved what had happened to him. He'd been so smug. So sure he could take from life exactly what he wanted without having to pay the price.

His brother had been right when he'd said Kyle was selfish. He *had* been selfish . . . for a long time.

Well, time had finally caught up with him.

His whole attitude had finally caught up with him.

And now, having discovered that what he thought he wanted from life wasn't what he wanted at all—it was too late.

He couldn't even stay angry with Rebecca. After all, she'd made her feelings clear from the beginning, just as he had with numerous women he'd dated through the years. Rebecca had done exactly what he'd been doing, but now the situations were reversed, and *he* was the one suffering.

A clean break.

Don't you agree? she'd asked.

A clean break was the last thing in the world he wanted. The thought of never seeing Rebecca again . . . never seeing his baby . . . was nearly intolerable.

Yet what choice did Kyle have but to honor Rebecca's edict?

Rebecca cried herself to sleep Friday night. But by Saturday morning, she was all cried out and quietly resigned. Tears would do her no good, she knew that. She had to face it. Her life was changing, going in a different direction than she would have preferred, but there was nothing she could do about it. And it was clearly not productive to dwell on what-might-have-beens.

For the sake of her baby, she had to be strong.

So she would move on. And she would not look back.

Saturday and Sunday she spent going through all of her belongings—deciding what she would take with her and what she would sell or give away. By immersing herself in physical activity, she managed—with only a few lapses—to keep her mind and heart free of Kyle.

Monday morning, first thing, she grabbed a cup of coffee and headed straight to Mark's office.

"Mark, you know how much I love working here."

"Oh, oh," he said, "this sounds serious."

Rebecca nodded. "I've decided to move back to Houston."

"I was afraid this might happen."

"Yes, I've just come to realize how much easier it will be for me to have my family close by. And it's much better to make the move now than after the baby comes." This was the approach she'd decided to take, because it was the most logical and one that was unarguable.

His smile was filled with regret. "Well, I can't say I'm not sorry. We're going to miss you."

"I'll miss the agency, too."

"Wait a minute. There's no reason for you to quit working for the agency. I'm sure Simon will be overjoyed to have you join the staff at the Houston office."

Rebecca had almost been afraid to hope this would be the case. "That would be wonderful."

"Tell you what," Mark said. "I'll give him a call this morning."

"I'd appreciate it, Mark."

"So," he said, leaning back in his chair, "how soon did you want to go?"

"As soon as possible. Say in two weeks?"

He shrugged. "That shouldn't be a problem. Later today I'll figure out who will be taking over your accounts, and as long as you can get them up to speed before you go, we should be in good shape."

Rebecca decided she would say nothing to her co-workers or her family until she'd heard whether she'd have a job in Houston. She didn't have long to wait. At eleven that morning, Simon Christopher called her.

"Rebecca," he said. "Mark tells me you want to come back to Houston."

"Yes," she said smiling, picturing Simon's friendly grin at the other end of the phone. He and his wife, Jenny, were two of her favorite people. She'd missed them after transferring to Cleveland.

"Boy, that couldn't be better for us. We were just saying the other day that we needed to hire another rep, and I was dreading it. It's always hard to train someone new, and now I won't have to."

"You're sure?"

"I'm positive. Mark says you'll be moving in a couple of weeks."

"I should be able to get there by July 1."

"But you'll need some time off to find a place to live."

"I'll live with my mother until I do. I don't want to use vacation since I'll be taking lots of time off when I have the baby." Suddenly Rebecca had a horrible thought. "Mark *did* tell you about the baby, didn't he?"

Simon chuckled. "Never fear. He told me. And I feel exactly the same way he does about it. You'll get three months' maternity leave just like anyone else. So don't worry about taking a few days' vacation when you move. I don't mind at all. Why don't you plan to start here after the Fourth of July holiday?"

As she had so many times before, Rebecca told herself how very lucky she was to have so many terrific friends and two such wonderful bosses.

Later she told her news to JoBeth.

"Oh, no!" JoBeth cried. "Tell me this is a joke."

Rebecca shook her head sadly. "It's not a joke."

"But *why?*"

"It'll just be so much easier for me to be close to my family. I haven't asked her yet, but I think my sister-in-law Miranda might be willing to watch the baby for me when I go back to work. She mentioned at Christmas that she was thinking of watching a child or two since she's stuck at home with a little one herself."

JoBeth slumped into one of the chairs in Rebecca's office. Her face was a picture of dismay. "I *hate* this," she said. "I'm going to miss you like crazy."

"I know. I'll miss you, too. But we can visit each other. You'll like Houston. It's a great place to visit."

JoBeth grinned. "Do I have to say 'y'all' and wear a cowboy hat if I come down there?"

Rebecca laughed. "No. Believe me, Houston is a very cosmopolitan city."

"But I *like* cowboy hats. I think I'd look good in one...*y'all*..." JoBeth batted her eyelashes.

Rebecca just shook her head at JoBeth's antics.

Throughout the rest of the afternoon, just as they had the day Rebecca had disclosed her pregnancy, the various members of the office staff stopped by her office to say how sorry they were to hear she was leaving. And with each new visitor, each knock at her door, Rebecca tensed, half-afraid it might be Kyle.

She knew she would probably have to see him again before she left Cleveland, but she hoped it wouldn't be today. She needed some time and distance. If she could get a few days behind her, she would be stronger and better able to face the eventual confrontation.

But the following day, in a special meeting where Mark assigned each of Rebecca's accounts to different reps, he also announced that Kyle would not be back in the Cleveland office again for several weeks. "He's taking some vacation to be with his grandfather, then he's going back to L.A. to try to get everything there in good shape before Brooke and I move out. In the meantime, I'll probably be dividing my time between here and there. Dell has agreed to be acting manager in my absence and until Kyle comes back full-time."

Rebecca received this news with conflicting feelings. So she wouldn't be seeing Kyle again. In some ways she was relieved, yet underlying the relief was an aching sadness and emptiness. She wondered if he had made the decision to stay away because he knew it would be easier for her if he did. Of course. That must be it. He was an innately thoughtful and generous man. His thoughtfulness and generosity were a large part of the reason she loved him so much.

Her heart beat in slow, heavy thuds as the import of Mark's words really sank in.

She would never see Kyle again.

Trembling inside, she excused herself from the meeting, murmuring something about the ladies' room. She stayed inside one of the stalls, away from prying eyes, until she'd managed to get herself under control again.

Then, dry-eyed and outwardly calm, she went out to face the world.

Kyle spent most of the day at the hospital. His grandfather had been moved from Coronary Care to a private room and looked about ten times better than he'd looked a few days earlier. There was color in his cheeks, his eyes looked clear and bright, and his voice sounded stronger.

"I hope I can go home in a day or so," he said.

"I hope so, too," Kyle said. "I've decided to take some vacation, and when you do go home, I'm going to stay at your house for a few days."

Graham's face lit up. "Thank you, Kyle. I'm very grateful you're willing to spend your vacation on an old man."

Guilt tugged at Kyle, and he wondered what his grandfather would say if he'd known the whole reason for his decision. Then he told himself the reasons didn't matter. What counted was his grandfather's pleasure and the fact that Kyle had made things easier for Rebecca, too. "It'll be great. Maybe you can finally teach me to play chess."

Now his grandfather beamed.

At least one good thing had come from Rebecca's decision to leave town, Kyle told himself later. He had made his grandfather very happy.

Lucy Taylor was overjoyed at Rebecca's news. "I can't wait. Oh, this is going to be so much fun."

Rebecca smiled. It was nice that out of such a difficult decision, someone was really happy.

Her brother John called the day after Rebecca had talked to her mother. "How are you planning to get all your things to Houston?" he said.

"I'm hiring a moving company."

"Good. Knowing you, I was afraid you might try to do too much yourself."

"John," Rebecca chided, "I'm not stupid."

"I know." After a second, he chuckled. "But you sure are stubborn."

Rebecca laughed, too. After all, her brother was right.

"We're all glad you're coming home," he said as their conversation wound to a close. "Shelley said to tell you she'll help you find a place to live when you're ready to strike out on your own again."

"I was counting on it." John's wife, Shelley, was a real-estate agent.

"Want me to fly up and drive back with you?"

"Oh, John, that's not necessary. I'm pregnant, not an invalid. But it was sweet of you to offer."

"What are brothers for," he teased, "if not to take care of little sisters?"

"Not so little anymore," Rebecca said, giving her expanding waistline a rueful look.

"Well, you be real careful driving. And we'll see you soon."

"Less than two weeks...."

The remainder of those two weeks seemed to fly by. Rebecca was so busy, both at home and at work, she didn't have time to brood about Kyle. Occasionally, though, her mind would rebel and turn inexorably in his direction, and at those times Rebecca didn't fight it. She figured she had to feel sad sometimes, and hopefully the sad times would slowly fade away. She hoped—prayed—that eventually all her memories of Kyle would be happy ones and she could pass those good recollections on to their son.

She did wonder how Kyle was doing. For some reason, no one in the office mentioned him to her, or talked about him, in her presence. At first, Rebecca wondered if people suspected something and that's why there was a conspiracy of silence. Gradually, though, she realized that Kyle had simply not called in or done anything to make people think much about him. For this she was grateful.

On Friday of the second week, her last day at work, Mark decreed that the office would shut down for two hours and let their answering service pick up messages while they all took Rebecca out for a farewell lunch.

They went to a popular downtown steakhouse where Mark had arranged for a private room. Rebecca was enormously touched to be presented with a hefty gift certificate as a going-away present. There were tears in her eyes as she hugged and kissed her co-workers goodbye.

"It's too bad Kyle couldn't be here," Chloe said.

"Yes," Rebecca agreed, but she was grateful he wasn't. It was hard enough to say these goodbyes without breaking down. With him there, it might have been impossible.

Later that day, JoBeth helped Rebecca pack up her personal belongings and two of the men carried them out to Rebecca's car.

After work, JoBeth followed Rebecca home. She had offered to help with the last-minute things that would need to be done before the movers arrived in the morning. About seven that night, they ordered a pizza, and Rebecca couldn't help but remember the last time JoBeth had eaten pizza in her house. She forced her mind away from the image.

At ten o'clock, JoBeth put down the roll of tape she'd been using and said, "That's it. The last box is taped and labeled, and you're ready to roll. I'm going to leave now, but I'll be back at seven to help you load up your car.''

"I don't know what I'd have done without you," Rebecca said. "Thank you."

"I'll get you back one of these days," JoBeth said.

The two women hugged, and JoBeth left.

Rebecca was so tired, she fell asleep immediately.

The next morning, true to her word, JoBeth arrived at seven sharp, bearing cups of coffee.

"Oh, you're a lifesaver!" Rebecca exclaimed. All of her kitchenware was packed.

"I even brought you decaf," JoBeth said.

The two women sat on the couch and drank their coffee and waited for the movers.

They arrived at nine. It only took them two hours to load all of Rebecca's belongings. As the truck moved down the hill on its way out of town, JoBeth and Rebecca hugged hard.

"Well, goodbye and lots of luck. I'm going to miss you so much." There was a catch in JoBeth's voice.

Rebecca's own eyes filled with tears and it was all she could do to keep from crying. "Come visit me soon," she whispered.

They kissed goodbye, then JoBeth, her smile only slightly off kilter, waved and left.

Twenty minutes later, Rebecca walked next door and handed her keys to Mrs. Andrews along with a check for a cleaning service to do a final cleaning of her half of the duplex, then she and Mariah—resigned to the cat carrier she hated—headed for Route 422 and Houston.

* * *

Graham MacNeill seemed to have a new lease on life. He improved rapidly during the two-week period following his release from the hospital. Kyle and his father had planned to hire a nurse to stay with him, but he was doing so well, Hugo said he thought he could manage without additional help. Kyle enjoyed the time with his grandfather. He learned to play a passable game of chess, they listened to music and they talked. All of this helped Kyle not think about Rebecca, although on her last day at the office, it was all he could do not to join her farewell lunch. He kept picturing her, wondering what she was thinking and doing, and he kept looking at the clock.

The day after Rebecca left for Houston, Kyle went back to Los Angeles. It only took him a couple of days to get things ready for Mark, and then he was on his way back to Cleveland, this time for good.

His first day back in the Cleveland office felt strange. Getting to work that morning, going into the kitchenette for coffee, all reminded him of so many other mornings when he'd carried that coffee into Rebecca's office.

Only, today Rebecca wasn't there. And she would never be there again. To keep from thinking about what that meant, he plunged into work. Work was the answer. Work and more work. And maybe, if he kept busy enough, he would eventually forget her.

Rebecca's family always had a huge cookout and family get-together at her mother's home for the Fourth of July, and this year was no exception.

Everyone was there: all of Rebecca's brothers and their wives and all of the nieces and nephews. Even Clem and Luke and their twins had managed to come, albeit at the last minute.

"Where'd you guys blow in from this time?" John said.

"Stockholm," Clem answered around a mouthful of peanuts.

"I didn't want to leave," Luke said, laughing. "Those Swedish women are gorgeous." He made a mock leer. "Did you know they sunbathe topless?"

James, who was Rebecca's youngest brother and a doctor, grinned. "I hope you took lots of pictures, Luke."

"He better not have! He told me he was photographing the archipelago while I was covering the election," Clem said.

"Where do you think all those women *do* their sunbathing?" Luke said.

Everyone laughed as Clem gave her husband a playful punch.

All of the commotion and good-natured teasing and conversation helped Rebecca forget about why she was there instead of in Cleveland. She was determined to forget, at least for today. Once the holiday was over and she reported to work, she knew there would be many painful reminders of everything she'd left behind, but today, just this one time, she wanted to enjoy herself.

It was too hot to stay outdoors for long—at least for Rebecca—so she wandered inside where she found her brother John's wife, Shelley, and Mark's wife, Miranda, in the kitchen with Lucy.

"Sit down, Rebecca. Join us," Miranda invited.

"I think I will. It's so hot out there."

Rebecca's mother, who was just putting the finishing touches to a plate of deviled eggs, turned and said, "And when you're pregnant, you feel the heat even worse than at other times."

"Are you excited about the baby?" Shelley asked, gray eyes friendly and curious.

Rebecca smiled. "Very." She really liked Shelley, an attractive blonde who had married John about a year and a half earlier. The entire family had been happy about the match because John's first wife, Cathy, had died of leukemia, and they'd all wanted to see John happy again.

"You're brave," Shelley said. "It's tough being a single parent. Believe me, I know. I was one for more than five years and there were times when I just wanted to sit down and cry."

"It's those middle-of-the-night feedings that really get to you," Miranda said.

"Well, she'll have me," Lucy said. Her green eyes, the exact color of Rebecca's, shone happily. "I'm looking forward to helping."

"You're so lucky," Shelley said. "My mother wasn't the least bit interested in helping out when Missy was born, and as for Missy's father, forget it."

Rebecca knew that Shelley's first marriage had been a disaster. Evidently her first husband had wanted a boy, and when they'd had a girl instead, he had turned his back on both her and his wife. "I *am* lucky," she said quietly. She'd been reminding herself of just how lucky every time she started to feel sad about Kyle, telling herself to focus on what she had and not on what she didn't have.

"I'm going to watch the baby for her when she goes back to work," Miranda said to Shelley.

"That's wonderful," Shelley said. "Good child care is so important."

"Have you decided on a name for the baby yet?" Miranda asked.

Rebecca shook her head. "No. I can't seem to make up my mind, but I'm leaning toward Jordan." What she really wanted was to name her son Graham, after Kyle's grandfather, but she was afraid someone—like JoBeth—might make some kind of connection and she knew she couldn't chance it.

"Jordan's a nice name," Shelley said.

"Yes, I like it," Miranda agreed. "What about you, Mom?" she said, addressing her question to Lucy.

Rebecca's mother smiled. "Jordan, Jordan," she said, testing the name. "Yes. I like it a lot."

"Good," Rebecca said. "Then that's settled." She patted her stomach. "Jordan it is."

Just then, the back door opened and Mark, the second oldest of Rebecca's brothers, came in carrying Robin, his and Miranda's two-year-old. Robin was rubbing her eyes and looked on the verge of crying.

"Here, Mom," Mark said, handing their daughter to Miranda, "someone is in desperate need of a nap."

Miranda stood. "I'm going to go upstairs and try to get her to sleep. Do you want to come with me, Rebecca?"

"Sure."

Rebecca's mother had converted one of the smaller bedrooms in the five-bedroom house into a permanent nursery. She'd said that with seven children she was sure she'd have heaps of grandkids, so a nursery was a necessity. Miranda sat in the rocking chair with the sleepy Robin and Rebecca sat on the window seat and watched them.

Miranda sang softly, smiling over Robin's head at Rebecca. Within minutes, Robin was asleep. Miranda laid her in the crib and covered her with a light blanket, because the air-conditioning kept the room cool. For a few moments, the two women stood looking down at the little girl.

"They're so sweet and innocent in sleep," Miranda whispered.

"Yes," Rebecca agreed. She touched her stomach. Soon she would have a child to rock to sleep.

"But, boy," Miranda said, "can they be a lot of work when they're not sleeping."

"I know."

Quietly they walked out of the room, and Miranda pulled the door partially shut. "They're worth all the work, though. They're worth anything you have to go through to have them."

Long after everyone else had left, Miranda's words echoed in Rebecca's mind.

The rest of July passed uneventfully for Rebecca. She was busy with her new job and seeing old friends and family. For the most part, she was content. But once in a while, something would happen that would remind her, with painful clarity, of what she'd never have.

One such time was a visit of Jenny Randall Christopher, the wife of Simon Christopher, Rebecca's boss, to the Houston office. She brought the children—dark-eyed, two-year-old Randall and blue-eyed, three-year-old Sarah. Seeing Simon's eyes light up, the way he unabashedly put his arm around Jenny and kissed her, the way he obviously doted on his adorable children, caused a lump to form in Rebecca's throat, and it was all she could do to keep her voice from trembling as she talked to Jenny.

Rebecca knew that Jenny and Simon had been best friends for many years and that it had taken Simon a long time to realize he loved Jenny. Simon had sheepishly admitted this was true. "Yeah, Jenny nearly gave up on me," he had said once, grimacing. "She had to practically hit me over the head to get my attention."

Jenny had laughed. "Actually, it was a handsome Frenchman paying attention to me that finally did it."

Rebecca thought about that conversation now. Even a handsome Frenchman paying attention to her wouldn't have made any difference with Kyle, she thought sadly. Because he wasn't dense. He was indifferent.

That night, Rebecca kept thinking about Jenny and Simon and the way they looked at each other. And the more she thought about them, the sadder and lonelier she felt. She kept touching her stomach, as if to reassure herself her baby was still there, although she could certainly feel him.

Finally, about eight o'clock, her mother said, "Rebecca, what's wrong?"

"Huh?" Rebecca looked up, startled. "N-nothing's wrong."

Lucy studied her silently for a few moments. "I know something's wrong. If you don't want to tell me, it's all right. But if I can, I want to help."

Without warning, Rebecca's eyes filled with tears, and no matter how hard she tried to keep them from falling, they spilled down her cheeks.

"Oh, darling, what is it?" Lucy moved to the couch and put her arms around Rebecca. "Please tell me."

"I—I..." Rebecca desperately tried to stop crying. But now that she'd started, it was as if someone had turned on a faucet.

"It's okay, it's okay," her mother said, patting Rebecca's head. "Just cry it all out, then we'll talk."

Rebecca allowed herself to be held and comforted. She, who had always chafed at what she called her family's "smothering," finally realized that some hurts are too big to carry alone. So, long minutes later, when her tears finally began to abate, she drew a long, shaky breath, blew her nose and said, "I lied to you."

Lucy's voice contained not a hint of censure as she said, "About what, sweetheart?"

Rebecca sighed. "I wasn't artificially inseminated." She looked at Lucy to see if her announcement had shocked her mother.

But Lucy only smiled sympathetically. "I always did doubt that story."

Chapter Fourteen

Rebecca stared at her mother. "You did? You never said anything."

"It wasn't my place to. I figured when and if you wanted to talk about it, you'd tell me."

Rebecca sighed deeply. "I want to tell you now, but you have to promise that you won't say anything to anyone else."

"Oh, darling, you know I won't."

So Rebecca told Lucy the whole story. Everything.

Lucy was quiet throughout Rebecca's recital. When Rebecca finished, Lucy said gently, "You love this man, don't you?"

"Yes." She swallowed. Why did it still hurt so much? Wouldn't she ever be free of this pain? "But he doesn't love me."

"Whether he loves you or not, he's still financially responsible for his child."

"I know. And he offered financial support, but I refused."

"Rebecca, that's not very smart."

"I don't care whether it's smart or not. It's the way I feel. If he doesn't love me, if he doesn't want to marry me and be a family...then I want nothing from him."

"But, darling—"

"No, Mother," Rebecca interrupted, "I don't want to argue the point. That's how I feel, and I'm not going to change my mind."

"But, Rebecca, this is *his* child you're carrying."

"But it was my idea to have this baby. He was against it, and I persuaded him. And I promised him he would not be obligated in any way."

"But if he *wants* to help you out...."

"No," Rebecca said firmly.

Her mother sighed, shoulders slumping in defeat.

"I'll be fine, Mother, really I will."

"I hope so," Lucy said, but her eyes contradicted her. They seemed to say, *but you're not fine now.*

Rebecca knew her mother was going to worry about her now, and she was almost sorry she'd confided in her. But later that night, after they'd both gone up to bed, as Rebecca lay looking at the shifting patterns the moonlight made on the ceiling, she decided she wasn't sorry, not really.

She'd needed to share the truth with someone and who better than her mother, the one person in the world who loved her unconditionally? At least now her burden would be easier to bear, so that maybe... finally... she could go wholeheartedly forward.

July would forever remain a blur in Kyle's mind. He worked like a man possessed, and when he wasn't working he was either at the gym giving his body a rigorous workout or at his grandfather's or working with the kids at the night basketball league.

He didn't date at all. Only one woman interested him, and she was in Houston.

Try as he might, he couldn't get Rebecca out of his mind. The trouble was, he thought ruefully, she had been such an integral part of his life and had shared so much with him, that everywhere he went and everything he did reminded him of her.

The office was the worst place, because he could hardly turn around without seeing something that triggered a memory of her.

And, of course, there were all the people in the office who were constantly asking about her or telling him something about her, so that even if he had managed to get through that particular day without thinking about her, his efforts were all shot to hell by their innocent comments.

One such time was a Friday night at the end of July. Kyle was hard at work when JoBeth poked her head into his office and said, "Hey, Kyle, did you hear the news about Rebecca?"

His heart jerked at her name, but his voice and expression were studiedly neutral as he answered. "What news?"

JoBeth walked in and perched on the corner of his desk. "I was just talking to Simon and he said Rebecca landed the Fisher Mills account."

Kyle whistled.

Fisher Mills was one of the biggest cereal and food-related companies in the nation. He knew they were unhappy with their longtime advertising agency and Simon had mentioned that they'd contacted Alonzo & Christopher and invited them to submit ideas, but that was all he knew. "No. I hadn't heard. That's great."

JoBeth's smile was quizzical. "I would've thought you'd be the first one she'd call."

He shrugged. "We haven't had a chance to talk much lately. We've both been really busy."

JoBeth nodded, but her dark eyes were speculative. "Did she tell you she's thinking about buying a house?"

"No. I, uh, haven't talked to her for a while." He was afraid JoBeth was going to keep asking him about Rebecca until it was obvious that something was wrong.

"Yeah, and if she buys a house, that means she'll never move back here."

Move back here? "Had she said she might move back?"

JoBeth shrugged. "No, but I was hoping...." She sighed. "Oh, well. I'm glad she's doing so well down there."

After JoBeth left, Kyle thought about the things she'd told him. He was glad Rebecca was doing well, too, even though he wished with all his heart she was still in Cleveland. He wondered how her pregnancy was going, if she felt well, if the baby was continuing to do well. If only he felt free to call her and ask her.

That night, in an effort to get his mind off Rebecca, he decided to go down to St. Rosco's, even though he normally didn't work with the boys on Friday nights. When he walked into the gym, he was glad to see Enos was there. He'd been wondering about the boy for days because Enos and Lisha and their parents had started counseling a week ago and Kyle was anxious to see how things had gone at their first couple of sessions.

"Mrs. Lambert, she's pretty nice," Enos said in answer to Kyle's question about how he liked the counselor.

"Good. I'm glad you like her." Kyle had set up and was paying for the appointments with the counselor, who was in private practice, because the state agencies were so overworked and the waiting lists were so long, Kyle was afraid Enos and his family might get discouraged and change their minds about going.

"You know, we talked about putting the baby up for adoption," Enos said, meeting Kyle's eyes briefly before looking away.

"How do you feel about that?"

Enos shrugged. "I don't know. At first I thought, yeah, that's cool, but then, the more I thought about it, I don't know." His dark eyes were troubled as they met Kyle's again. "I mean, that baby, I'm starting to feel like it's mine, man, you know what I mean?" Before Kyle could answer, he added, "You prob'ly don't, 'cause you don't have any kids."

Kyle would have been ashamed to have anyone know that Enos's words produced a swift stab of envy.

But Kyle couldn't seem to help the way he felt. Here they were, two men of different ages, races, backgrounds and prospects for the future, and Enos, who was the disadvantaged one in all these categories, had the freedom and the right to claim his child as his own and have a part in the decisions regarding that child's future.

Whereas Kyle seemed to have no rights at all when it came to his own unborn child.

That night, he lay awake for a long, long time.

"Rebecca, why don't you just stay here until after the baby is born?"

Rebecca looked up from the morning newspaper, which she'd been reading while eating her breakfast. "I have been thinking about it," she admitted.

"Then do," Lucy said eagerly.

"I don't know. I'm afraid it might be too much for you. After all, you're working now." Rebecca's mother had started working for the family's security business a few years ago and loved it.

"Why would my working make a difference?"

"Mom, you've obviously forgotten, although with seven children I don't know how you could," Rebecca said dryly, "but little babies do a lot of crying in the night. It's pretty hard to get a decent night's sleep." She speared the last bite of pancakes on her plate and ate them.

"My bedroom is at the other side of the house from yours," her mother pointed out. "The baby won't bother me."

"Gee, I don't know." But it was certainly tempting to take her mother up on her offer, although it amazed

Rebecca that she wanted to. She, who had always been so independent, so determined to do things on her own, had reverted to childhood and was actually happy to have her mother taking care of her. Rebecca studied her mother's eager face. "Are you sure you want me? You don't just feel sorry for me, do you?"

"Honey, I'd be thrilled to have you stay for a while." Lucy smiled. "To tell you the truth, I've missed having a baby around."

"Well..."

"It's settled," Lucy said happily. "You're staying."

Rebecca reminded herself once again of how lucky she was. Even so, she couldn't help but think what it might be like to bring a new baby home to the house you shared with your husband instead of to the house you shared with your mother.

She wondered how Kyle was doing. Although she talked to JoBeth a couple of times a week, all JoBeth had said was, "He's turned into a workaholic. Comes early. Stays late. Works on weekends."

Did he ever think about her? Rebecca wondered. Did he ever think about their baby?

In the first days after she'd moved back to Houston, she'd half expected him to call her. She'd even rehearsed what she would say, how she would remind him that he'd agreed to a clean break. Then, when he *didn't* call, she'd been perversely disappointed and hurt.

You've gotten exactly what you said you wanted, she lectured herself—Kyle's baby and a clean break. What is your problem?

The problem was, she finally admitted one soul-searching night when she couldn't sleep, that she had lied to herself. And like any lie, it had consequences. Consequences she was now having to pay for and would continue having to pay for for the rest of her life.

Kyle's grandfather continued to get stronger through the month of August, and by mid-September he looked to be in better shape than he had been in years. Kyle was grateful. For however long this good period lasted, he was glad to have it.

Work was going well, too.

The only thing not going well was his personal life. It was still a shambles. He'd expected that as time went on, he would stop missing Rebecca so much. Instead, as each day passed, he seemed to miss her more.

Take that day—it was a Friday. That morning he'd presided over the weekly staff meeting. During the discussions of various accounts, Rebecca's name had come up several times. A couple of people had mentioned talking to her, and Kyle hadn't been able to shake the feeling of depression that their comments had precipitated.

The urge to call her was getting stronger every day. He kept telling himself he couldn't. He had promised. She wanted a clean break, and he'd agreed. Several times he had even picked up the phone, only to replace it angrily. No, he told himself, he would not call her. She wanted nothing more to do with him. He wasn't going to force himself on her. After all, he had his pride.

* * *

"What's wrong, Kyle?" his grandfather asked him one night in early October.

"Wrong? Nothing's wrong. What makes you ask?" Kyle mentally kicked himself for giving in to the weakness of thinking about Rebecca, especially in his grandfather's shrewd-eyed company.

"Oh," Graham said dryly, "nothing much. Only the fact that you seem to be preoccupied most of the time and no longer seem to be having any fun."

That about summed it up, Kyle thought. "I have had a lot on my mind," he admitted. "It's not easy taking over an office where you were once just one of the guys. There've been a lot of problems." This was an exaggeration, but it was an explanation Kyle felt his grandfather would accept.

"I think it's more than that," Graham said. "I think something's bothering you—something that has nothing to do with work."

Kyle shrugged and decided to tell as much of the truth as possible. "I can't fool you, can I? I *have* been a little depressed. Fact is, I've been dealing with a disappointing personal relationship. Someone I was seriously interested in wasn't interested in me."

"I find that hard to believe."

"It's the truth."

Graham frowned. "Who is this woman? Is she crazy?"

Kyle wanted to smile, even though there was nothing to smile about where Rebecca was concerned. Still, it was flattering to see how much his grandfather thought of him. "No," he said quietly, "she's not crazy."

"Well, there are other fish in the sea," Graham staunchly pronounced. "The thing to do when you've had a disappointing love affair is to go right out and find someone new."

Kyle nodded. "I know, but, well, I'm finding it hard to forget about her." He met his grandfather's gaze and something about the old man's expression shattered the wall around Kyle's emotions. "You see, she's the only woman I've ever really loved, and I didn't realize it until it was too late."

"I don't understand."

"I know. I'm just beginning to understand myself," Kyle said slowly. "The thing is, I...took her for granted for a long time. I think I might have had a chance to win her love, but by the time I finally realized that was what I wanted, she had moved on."

"Did you tell her how you feel?"

"No, I told you. It was too late."

"But if you didn't tell her, how do you know she wasn't interested?"

"I can't explain it, but trust me, I know."

Graham was silent for a long time. Finally he said, "Kyle, I might be an old man, and I might not know how things are done today, but I do know that there are some things that never change. There is no way you can know what is in a woman's heart unless you ask her. And there is no way for her to know what is in your heart unless you tell her."

There is no way you can know what is in a woman's heart unless you ask her. And there is no way for her to know what is in your heart unless you tell her....

Kyle thought and thought about all the conversations he'd had with Rebecca over the past months. He thought particularly hard about the conversation in which he'd said he wanted to have a part in the up-bringing of their child.

You never really said that.

What had he said? He'd offered financial support, and he'd said he wanted to do the right thing. But he hadn't told Rebecca he loved her, and he hadn't told her he wanted to marry her.

Should he call her?

Should he try again, this time being completely honest with her?

What did he have to lose?

Only your pride.

He held out until the third week of October. Then, late that Friday afternoon, he picked up the phone and dialed the Houston office number.

"Hi," he said to the unrecognizable voice who answered the phone, "this is Kyle MacNeill."

"Uh, hello," the girl said. "Um, can I help you?"

Kyle realized she didn't know who he was. "Where's Cherry?" Cherry had been the receptionist at the Houston office for years and knew everyone in the company.

"Um, she's on vacation. Can you hold, please?"

"Sure, I—" But the girl cut him off midsentence. Kyle impatiently tapped his pen. Obviously, this was a temp filling in and she was rattled by the busy switchboard.

"Hello, Mr. MacNeill?" The girl was back, sounding more harried than ever. "How can I help you?"

"Well, I manage the Cleveland office of the company," Kyle began.

"Oh, I'm sorry."

"That's okay. I'd like to speak to Rebecca Taylor."

"Oh, sorry, she's not here. She had to go to the hospital. Something to do with the baby." In the background, Kyle could hear other lines ringing. "Hold on again, please," the distracted girl said and cut him off.

Kyle stared at the dead phone. Rebecca had had to go to the hospital! Something to do with the baby. Something must be wrong. His heart pounded in fear.

He pushed the redial button for the Houston office. The phone rang and rang and rang. "Dammit to hell!" He banged the receiver down, then turned to his computer. Hurriedly he keyed in the commands for the company's data base, then brought up the file on all the employees. He knew, from office gossip, that Rebecca was living with her mother. He scrawled the information on a scrap of paper, then decided he would at least try to call her mother's house. Maybe someone would be there and be able to give him information on what hospital Rebecca had gone to.

But all he got at her mother's number was an answering machine. He didn't leave a message.

At eleven o'clock the following morning, he strode up the Jetway into Houston Intercontinental Airport's Terminal C. He headed straight for the rental car desk.

Fifteen minutes later, a Houston map and his one carryon in hand, he was on a shuttle heading for the remote lot.

A few minutes after twelve-thirty, he arrived at the stately brick house on Houston's northwest side. It had been easy to find. He parked in front, even though the driveway was clear of vehicles, then walked slowly up the front walk and rang the doorbell. While he waited, he looked around. It was a pleasant street, filled with mature trees and well-tended lawns and nicely aged homes. A good place to grow up.

His stomach jumped with nerves. Ever since yesterday afternoon, he'd called and called here at Rebecca's mother's, with no success. He had finally decided that he would just come to Houston and camp out on their doorstep until someone came home. He could think of no other way to find out what was going on without alerting Simon or someone else in the office to his specific interest in her.

And Kyle couldn't do that to Rebecca. Not unless she agreed.

He rang the doorbell again, then peered in through the diamond-shaped bevel glass panel in the door. He saw an empty entrance hall and no sign of life. Just as he turned, disappointed and frustrated, a tall woman with faded blond hair rounded the corner of the house.

"Hello," she said. "I *thought* I heard the doorbell. I was out back, working in the flower beds."

Kyle took in her appearance as she walked closer: the gardening gloves and trowel, the green eyes so like Rebecca's, the warm smile. "Hi. You must be Mrs. Taylor."

"Yes. And you are...?"

"Kyle MacNeill, a friend of Rebecca's."

"Oh." Her eyes studied him thoughtfully.

Kyle wondered if she knew anything about him. Would Rebecca have confided in her mother? She hadn't before leaving Cleveland, but maybe, living here, she might have. Kyle wished he knew.

"I'm afraid Rebecca's not here," she said.

"I know. I called the office late yesterday afternoon, and they told me she'd gone to the hospital. That's why I'm here. I—has she had the baby? Is everything all right?" He couldn't keep the worry out of his voice, even though he tried.

Lucy Taylor gave him a funny look, then she smiled. "She hasn't had the baby yet. It's not due for another ten days."

"I know, but they said—"

"She just had to go for a checkup."

"A checkup? But why did she go to the hospital?"

"Because her doctor's office is there."

Kyle felt like a fool.

"Come on," Lucy said. "Let's go in the house. You look like you need to sit down."

Ten minutes later, Kyle found himself sitting at the kitchen table with a fat ham sandwich and a tall glass of iced tea in front of him and Lucy Taylor's kind face opposite him.

"You're the baby's father, aren't you?" she said.

He nodded wearily, not the least bit surprised that she knew the truth.

"You know," she said, "I thought if I ever had the chance to talk to you, I'd give you a piece of my mind for making my daughter so unhappy, but I can see you're unhappy, too."

"I've never been more miserable in my life," Kyle admitted.

"You love Rebecca, don't you?"

"Yes."

"What do you plan to do about it?"

"All I can do is tell her how I feel."

Lucy's smile lit up her face. "Well, you don't have long to wait, because I think I hear her car in the driveway now."

Chapter Fifteen

Rebecca idly wondered whose car was parked in front of her mother's house. Must be someone visiting next door. Dismissing the thought, she pulled into the driveway. Her stomach rumbled, and she grinned. She was hungry. Lately, she was always hungry.

She was also tired, but pleasantly so. She'd been gone most of the morning, running errands and buying last-minute supplies for the eminent arrival of her son. It would be nice to go inside, have some lunch, then lay down for a nap. Her mother kept telling her to pamper herself, "because you won't get much sleep after the baby comes."

Gathering up her packages, Rebecca got out of the car and walked to the back door. It was a beautiful day, the kind of day she loved most—in the low seventies, clear and sunny, with a slight breeze that ruffled the leaves on the stately oaks shading the backyard. It was a nice yard. Lucy loved working outside, and she did a good job of maintaining the flower beds and keeping the shrubs trimmed.

Actually, it looked as if Lucy had been working in the yard this morning. The flower beds bordering the back of the house were freshly weeded and watered, and some of Lucy's gardening tools were laying nearby. Rebecca frowned slightly. It wasn't like her mother to leave things lying around like that. She must have been interrupted and forgotten about them.

Rebecca shuffled her packages so that she could open the back door, which led through the utility room and then into the big kitchen/den combination. When she opened the door, her mother was standing there with a funny look on her face.

"Hi," Rebecca said. She dumped her packages on the kitchen table and saw that her mother must have just fixed herself some lunch, for there was a ham sandwich and glass of iced tea sitting there. "I hope there's more ham, because I'm starving."

"There's plenty of ham."

There was an odd kind of lilt to her mother's voice. Rebecca gave her a quizzical smile, wondering if something had happened. "Is something wrong?"

Lucy smiled. "No, no, nothing's wrong."

"Well, good, because I'm not only hungry, I'm tired. After lunch, I think I'll take a nap." She walked to the refrigerator and opened the meat keeper.

"Rebecca . . ."

"Hmm?" Rebecca, package of ham in hand, turned.

"Before you make your sandwich, go into the living room. There's, uh, something there I want you to see."

Rebecca smiled. "A baby present?"

Lucy's eyes were shining. "You might say that...."

Bemused, Rebecca put down the package of ham and slowly walked to the front of the house. The living room was flooded with sunlight, and for a second, she saw nothing. Then, causing her heart to skyrocket, Kyle moved into her line of vision.

She gasped. Blinked. The thought flitted through her mind that she was hallucinating.

And then he spoke. "Hello, Rebecca."

"Kyle," she breathed. Her heart was still going like a piston, and her knees felt weak. She grasped at the back of a leather wing chair, her mind still trying to take in what her eyes were telling her. "Wh-what are you doing here?" She felt battered by the turbulence of her emotions.

"I came because I had to see you."

"I—I think I have to sit down."

He immediately rushed forward, taking her arm and leading her to the couch. "I'm sorry. I don't know what I was thinking of. Here. Sit down."

Rebecca was trembling all over as the full impact of Kyle's presence hit her. He sat beside her and took her hand in his. His eyes were filled with concern. Why had he come? she wondered. Was something wrong?

"Don't look so frightened," he said softly.

She wet her lips. "Please, Kyle, what is it? Why did you have to see me?"

His hand tightened around hers. "Because I've been such a fool. Because there's something I should have told you before you left Cleveland. Something that I hope is going to make a difference.''

"What?" Rebecca whispered, mesmerized by the look in his eyes.

His eyes looked deep into hers. "That I love you."

At first, Rebecca was sure she'd imagined the words, just as she'd thought she'd imagined his physical presence.

And then he said them again. "I think I've always loved you, but I was just too blind to see it."

Rebecca's eyes filled with tears. "Oh, Kyle..."

"Is there any hope for me?"

Laughing and crying at the same time, Rebecca threw her arms around his neck. "Yes, yes, there's hope. I love you, too. I have for a very long time."

He kissed her then. A bells-ringing, toes-tingling, fireworks-exploding kind of kiss that warmed every cold place in Rebecca's heart and shot her up into the stars where everything was bright and beautiful and magical. He kept kissing her and whispering how much he loved her, and Rebecca's head spun with the dizzying sweetness of it all.

Afterward, he tucked her head under his chin and held her close.

He laid his hand gently on her stomach. "I'm sorry it took me so long to come to my senses, but I have now." Tipping her chin up, he looked at her tenderly. "Will you marry me, Rebecca?"

"Oh, yes, yes, I'll marry you." Rebecca wasn't sure she could take so much happiness at one time.

They kissed again. And again.

"I've missed you so much," Kyle whispered.

"I've missed you, too."

"I have so much to make up for. But I will make it up to you. I promise."

After a bit, Rebecca said, in the time-honored tradition of all lovers, "What happened to make you realize you loved me?"

Kyle's smile was indulgent. "What happened? My life felt so empty. Nothing really made me happy and nothing really interested me. It finally dawned on me that the reason I felt that way was because you weren't there. After that, it didn't take a genius to figure out that I loved you and probably had for a long time."

Rebecca sighed with happiness.

Just then, the baby kicked.

"Kyle, feel," she said, placing his hand back on her stomach. She watched his face as the baby kicked again, then again.

Kyle's eyes widened in wonder. "He's kicking!"

"Yes."

"Wow."

They smiled at each other.

"I haven't even asked how you're feeling," Kyle said.

"I'm feeling wonderful. I went to the doctor yesterday."

"I know," he said ruefully. "I called the office."

Rebecca chuckled when he told her about the temporary receptionist and how she'd scared him. "Is that why you came? Because you got scared?"

"That was just the excuse I gave myself. I'd been trying to work up the courage to come for days."

"Work up your courage?" Rebecca teased. "Am I so frightening that you needed courage to come and see me?"

He kissed her forehead. "If you'd thrown me out, I wouldn't have been surprised." His voice sobered. "I'm not ashamed to admit it. I was scared out of my mind that you'd tell me to get lost."

Rebecca didn't know how one person could stand to be so happy. "I think I'll send that temp some flowers," she said.

"No, *I'll* send her some flowers."

They both laughed.

A little while later, Kyle said, "How many days does it take to get a marriage license in Texas?"

"I'm not sure. Three, I think."

"Is the office where you apply for one open on Saturdays?"

"Probably not. Why?"

"Well, I was thinking, if it was, we could go down there now and apply for it, and if it's a three-day waiting period, that means we could get married on Tuesday."

"Oh, Kyle, I'm not sure we could get everything ready by Tuesday."

"Ready? What's to get ready? All we need is a license and two witnesses and a justice of the peace." He patted her stomach. "After all, we don't have much time before our son gets here."

"But Kyle, I don't want to be married by a J.P. I want to be married in church, in a white dress, carrying flowers and surrounded by my family and friends. And I want Luke to give me away. I'm not sure he could even get here by Tuesday. In fact, I'm not sure where he is right now."

"But, Rebecca, our baby is coming. Don't you want to be married before he's born?"

"Yes, but we can still make it. We can go down Monday and apply for our license, and if I put my mother and sisters-in-law to work on it, I think we can get everything together so that we can be married by next Saturday." She grinned. "That'll still give us three or four days before Junior here is due. That's long enough for a honeymoon, isn't it?"

"The rest of our life is going to be a honeymoon," he said, nuzzling his mouth against her neck.

A delicious shiver raced down Rebecca's spine. She closed her eyes and gave herself up to another soul-searing kiss that left them both breathless.

"I want you," he whispered.

"I know."

"Do you want me?"

"Very, very much."

"I'm not sure I can wait a week."

Rebecca pulled back. She looked into his eyes. "Kyle," she said softly, "I know we've been pretty unconventional up until now, but from this moment on, I want everything about the rest of our lives to be traditional. I want us to wait and…and not make love again until we're husband and wife. And I want our wedding day to be beautiful and special and something we'll remember for the rest of our lives."

He laid his forehead against hers. "All right, you win. Next Saturday it is."

Rebecca took his hand. "Let's go tell my mother."

Lucy wasted no time. An hour after Rebecca and Kyle walked into the kitchen hand in hand, she was on the phone calling their minister. She made a thumbs-up sign in the middle of the conversation. "We've got the church for next Saturday afternoon," she said gleefully. "And we'll all come back here afterward."

That night, Rebecca called JoBeth and Kyle called his grandfather.

"I want you to be my maid of honor," Rebecca told JoBeth.

JoBeth was, at first, speechless. Then, chuckling, she said, "Rebecca, you're a deep one. I would have never guessed. Not in a million years. And Kyle, that's *really* a shocker. God, when I think how many women tried to land him and couldn't." She made an odd sound. "Including me, I'll admit it."

So Rebecca's hunch had been right. "I never knew that," she said.

"Yeah, I was freshly divorced and made a play for him, but don't worry, he never gave me the time of day."

"JoBeth, I hope this doesn't—"

"I said, don't worry about it. It wasn't Kyle's fault he wasn't interested in me, and I don't hold it against him. And I certainly don't hold it against you. I mean it, Rebecca, I'm thrilled for you."

"Good. I'd feel terrible if this made a difference to our friendship."

"Nothing will ever make a difference to our friendship."

Smiling and relieved, Rebecca told her to bring a dress with her. "It can be any color, as long as it's suitable for a church wedding."

JoBeth said she'd be there no later than Thursday. "I'll call you and let you know what flight I'll be on."

Kyle's grandfather was equally thrilled and was practically ecstatic when Kyle told him about the baby.

"I'm coming down for the wedding," he announced, "and staying until the newest MacNeill shows up, too."

"You know I'd love to have you, but is it a good idea?" Kyle said. "You're still recuperating, and all the excitement and everything . . ."

"It isn't every day my favorite grandson gets married and has a child. I'm coming," Graham said emphatically, "and that's that."

Next, Kyle called his parents. "They're both coming," he told Rebecca. "This is going to be interesting. They haven't spoken a civil word in months."

On Sunday, every member of Rebecca's family who was in town came over to Lucy's house to meet Kyle. Rebecca grinned when each one of her brothers, in turn, gave Kyle the third degree. He held up well, and Rebecca could see that by the end of the day, he'd won them all over.

On Monday, Rebecca and Kyle—who had set up his base of operations in a nearby hotel where he'd taken a suite—went downtown to the courthouse to apply for their marriage license.

Monday afternoon, leaving Kyle to spend a few hours with Simon in the Houston Office, Rebecca and her mother went looking for a wedding dress.

The first maternity shop they tried had nothing suitable, but the young salesclerk, who lowered her voice so the owner wouldn't hear her, said, "Have you tried that new store at Willowbrook? It's much bigger, and I'll bet you'll be able to find something there."

The saleswoman at the shop at Willowbrook smiled and said, "I think I've just the thing." She led Re-

becca over to a section of cocktail dresses and evening gowns. "You're in luck, because we just got our
holiday shipment in." Reaching up, she brought out a
beautiful off-white lace cocktail dress fashioned with
an empire waist banded with white satin and a scal-
loped hemline.

"Oh," Rebecca said, "it's perfect." She took it into
the dressing room to try it on.

"Yes," Lucy said, blinking back tears as she looked
at Rebecca, "it *is* perfect. You look beautiful, darling."

After buying the dress, they purchased a veil and
creamy satin pumps with tiny rosettes. Afterward,
they were so pleased with themselves, they splurged on
chocolate milkshakes and cheeseburgers at Wendy's.

With the hurdles of a church and a dress taken care
of, Rebecca figured she could handle anything.

The rest of the week was a beehive of activity and
excitement. On Monday night, Rebecca and Lucy took
turns calling everyone, since there was no time for
formal invitations. On Tuesday, they engaged a ca-
terer who promised she could deliver both the kind of
meal Lucy wanted to serve the guests as well as the
wedding cake Rebecca wanted.

On Wednesday, a cleaning service came in and
cleaned the house from top to bottom while Rebecca
and Kyle spent the day shopping for rings and arrang-
ing for flowers and finding a photographer who was
willing to work on such short notice.

They had a romantic, candlelight dinner at Bren-
nan's that night, and afterward they went back to
Kyle's hotel so they could indulge in a little necking in

private. "But no more than necking," Rebecca warned, laughing.

"You're a hard woman," Kyle grumbled.

On Thursday, JoBeth arrived. She hugged Rebecca hard. "I'm happy for you," she said. "I don't know why you want to marry this guy, but I'm happy for you." She gave Kyle a mock punch.

Kyle laughed. "I don't know why she wants to marry me, either, but I sure am glad."

JoBeth had brought a beautiful emerald green taffeta cocktail dress with an off-the-shoulder neckline to wear for the wedding, and Rebecca declared it perfect.

Later Thursday, Kyle's mother arrived. Rebecca had been nervous about meeting her, but she needn't have worried. Gwen MacNeill was just as warm and charming as Kyle, and she and Rebecca immediately hit it off. "You didn't tell me about this," she said, indicating Rebecca's pregnancy and giving Kyle a stern look.

Kyle's smile was sheepish. "I didn't want to get into it on the telephone."

On the way to the hotel, he explained.

"Men," Gwen MacNeill said, exchanging a look with Rebecca. "They can be really dense sometimes."

Rebecca just smiled.

On Friday, Kyle's grandfather came, accompanied by the ever-faithful Hugo and Kyle's father. Both the senior MacNeills hugged Rebecca and patted Kyle on the back.

"Is your mother here?" Donald asked, turning to Kyle.

"Yes," said Kyle. "And I expect the two of you to act like mature adults."

"I hope you told her that," Donald grumbled.

"Look, Dad," Kyle said, "this is my wedding, and I don't want it spoiled."

"Fine, fine," Donald said.

"It better be fine."

A few hours later, just barely in time for the rehearsal, Clem and Luke and their twins arrived. Clem said she'd stay home with the children while Luke accompanied Rebecca and JoBeth to the church. "I'll meet you at the restaurant later," she said. Kyle was hosting the rehearsal dinner at one of Rebecca's favorite Mexican restaurants in an effort to give the out-of-town visitors a taste of local flavor.

The rehearsal went off without a hitch. Rebecca had been worried about what Reverend Jamison would think or perhaps say when he saw the advanced state of her pregnancy, but except for a slight frown, he expressed no disapproval.

The rehearsal dinner also proceeded smoothly, the only iffy moment occurring when Donald MacNeill balked at sitting next to his former wife at the head table. But after a hard look from Kyle, Donald sat and even managed to exchange a few words with Gwen without them erupting into an argument.

Afterward, Kyle and Rebecca had a short time alone when he drove her back to her mother's house. He pulled up in front and cut the lights and ignition. "I can't wait until tomorrow," he said, pulling her into his arms and kissing her softly. He caressed her stomach. "I still can't believe it. I'm going to be a husband and days later, a father."

Rebecca smiled and thanked God for all her blessings.

Rebecca's wedding day dawned bright and beautiful, with clear blue skies and the promise of warm breezes. She awoke early because she'd had a hard time sleeping comfortably. Her back was really aching, and she imagined that was because she'd been doing too much in the past few days.

After showering and dressing, she headed downstairs where she found her mother already up and drinking coffee.

"Happy wedding day, darling," Lucy said.

"Thanks, Mom." Rebecca walked over to her mother and put her arms around her, laying her head against her mother's. "I love you," she said softly. "Thanks for everything."

"I love you more," Lucy said. "And you're very welcome."

About thirty minutes later, a still-sleepy-eyed Jo-Beth joined them, saying, "Coffee, coffee . . ."

Soon after that Clem and Luke and the twins came down, and the morning quiet disappeared. After that, the activity in the house escalated. Flowers came. Food came. Presents were delivered. Trucks backed in and out of the driveway.

Rebecca decided to get out of the way. She wasn't feeling wonderful, anyway, so she went upstairs to the little sitting room her mother had fashioned and put her feet up and stuffed a pillow behind the small of her back and surfed through the TV channels until she found an old Katherine Hepburn movie.

At noon she went downstairs to find a big pot of mushroom soup was on the stove and tuna fish sandwiches were piled on a platter in the center of the table. She really wasn't very hungry, but her mother insisted she eat something, so she placated her by having a bowl of soup.

After lunch it was no time at all before Rebecca and the rest of the family needed to begin to get ready. The wedding was to take place at three o'clock.

Rebecca had hoped her backache would go away, but it seemed to get worse as the day wore on. By the time JoBeth was helping her to dress, Rebecca was wincing from the pain.

JoBeth frowned. "What's wrong?"

"Um, just bad back pain," Rebecca said.

"Oh, God, you're not starting labor, are you?"

"Oh, no, no, nothing like that. It's just that I've been doing too much this past week. My back is suffering for it."

When they joined the rest of the family downstairs, Lucy's eyes filled with tears.

"Now don't get all weepy, Mom," Rebecca said, "or I'll start crying, too."

Lucy laughed and brushed away the tears.

Rebecca thought her mother looked wonderful. She was wearing a peach crepe suit with rhinestone-and-pearl buttons and a matching pillbox hat.

Luke wore a black tux and Clem looked striking in black and white. And the twins! They looked adorable, Rebecca thought, grinning down at them. Lucas and Lee Ann looked more like their mother than their father, with their dark hair and bright faces, but they inherited Luke's eyes—the same green shot with gold that were a Taylor family trademark. Little Lucas wore a navy blazer and gray slacks with a white shirt and bow tie, and Lee Ann wore a taffeta dress in black, red and white plaid.

"We sure are a handsome group," she said.

They left for the church at two-thirty. During the drive, the pain in Rebecca's back was constant, but now it was joined by a cramping feeling in her stomach that came and went. The fear she'd had earlier but had denied to JoBeth returned. What if she were starting labor? She wondered if she should say anything, but she didn't want to get everyone all excited. Even if she *were* starting labor, this first phase went on for quite a while, according to the book she'd been reading. There would be plenty of time to get through the wedding ceremony and probably even the reception before she had to go to the hospital.

She clutched her flowers tighter and told herself to take deep breaths and relax.

"You okay?" JoBeth said from the seat next to her. Her brown eyes were flecked with concern.

Rebecca smiled reassuringly. "I'm fine. It's just nerves."

"You sure? You still having pain?"

"A little."

"Oh, God, maybe I should tell—"

"No," Rebecca whispered. She didn't want Luke, who was driving, to hear them. "Don't tell my mother. Don't tell anyone. Don't worry, either. I'm going to be fine. It's not labor." *It's not labor. It's not. I won't let it be labor. I have to get married first.*

They pulled up in front of the church to find a throng of well-dressed people milling around outside.

Among them Rebecca spied her younger brother, James, talking animatedly to a pretty dark-haired girl who must be his latest flame. The rest of Rebecca's family must already be inside, she decided.

"What time is it?" she said, ignoring another clutch of pain low in her stomach, which radiated around to her back and seemed to last a bit longer than the one preceding it. *It's not labor.*

"Ten minutes till three," Luke said from the driver's seat. He cut the ignition, got out and opened the passenger side door. JoBeth exited. Then he came around to open the door on Rebecca's side, which faced the church. Smiling down at her, he helped her out.

The pain had subsided, and Rebecca was able to smile back wholeheartedly.

People oohed and aahed and smiled at her as she made her way through them and into the vestibule. Within moments, all of the people from outside entered the church and were seated. JoBeth squeezed Rebecca's hand as Rebecca's brother John escorted Lucy down the aisle.

"Ready?" Luke said.

"Oh, I'm ready," Rebecca said just as another pain speared her. She hoped JoBeth wouldn't notice her quick intake of breath or her involuntary wince.

"Another one, huh?" JoBeth muttered close to Rebecca's ear.

Rebecca nodded.

"Oh, boy," JoBeth said.

"We'll make it," Rebecca assured her.

She took a deep breath as the strains of "The Wedding March" filled the air.

"Good luck," JoBeth whispered. Then she walked to the center aisle and began the hesitation step toward the altar.

Luke held out his left arm, and Rebecca took it. Her heart picked up speed as they moved to follow JoBeth down the aisle.

The church looked beautiful. It was an old church with lovely stained-glass windows that turned the sunlight streaming through them into a rainbow of jewel tones that lay softly on the gleaming walnut pews and the heads and faces of the expectant guests.

But Rebecca only had eyes for Kyle: a gorgeous Kyle in a gleaming black tux, blue eyes shining as he watched her progress down the aisle. His father was acting as his best man, and he, too, smiled at Rebecca.

Halfway down the aisle, another pain hit, this one so sharp, Rebecca stumbled. She recovered quickly, but she could hardly breathe. It was at that moment that she knew she was definitely in labor. She told herself it would all be fine, she would make it through the wedding, but she was scared. The pains seemed to be so close together.

Still, she managed to keep her smile from slipping, and she managed to get to the altar. She even managed to take Kyle's hand and go up the three shallow steps to face Reverend Jamison.

But just as he finished saying, "Dearly beloved, we are gathered here today to witness the marriage of Rebecca Elaine Taylor and Kyle Graham MacNeill," she was hit with another contraction, this one so hard and so sharp, she doubled over and would have fallen if Kyle hadn't grabbed her.

Afterward, Kyle could laugh about it. But when it happened, all he felt was panic. Rebecca, her eyes big as saucers, gasped, "Oh, Kyle, the baby's coming," and after that, all hell broke loose.

Reverend Jamison said, "Oh, dear."

Donald MacNeill said, "Oh, damn."

JoBeth said, "Oh, no, I was afraid of this," and rushed forward to help Kyle support Rebecca.

Lucy Taylor jumped up, and the assembled guests were all talking at once, and someone said—Kyle thought it was Luke—"We've got to get her to the hospital!"

Between Kyle and Luke and Lucy and JoBeth, they managed to get Rebecca into the car, with Luke to do the driving because Kyle didn't know the way. Lucy said, "I'm going, too," and climbed in with them.

Rebecca's other brothers said they'd go to the house and entertain the guests.

"I'll call you," Lucy promised.

Reverend Jamison and JoBeth, in a car driven by Donald MacNeill, followed closely behind the car containing Rebecca.

Kyle was frantic. He held Rebecca's hand tightly and grimaced along with her as her pains seemed to come faster and faster.

Rebecca tried to remember what she'd been told by her doctor. She knew she should take shallow breaths, but it was hard. "Please hurry," she said at one point.

They reached the hospital in record time, the car with JoBeth and Reverend Jamison right behind.

The hospital personnel took in the situation quickly, and a wheelchair was produced. So Rebecca, in her wedding finery and still carrying her flowers, accompanied by Kyle who was still holding her hand tightly, her mother, Luke and JoBeth, was wheeled inside, and all the while, Reverend Jamison scuttled along behind, hastily saying the words of the wedding ceremony.

Other patients, visitors, nurses, doctors and hospital workers all stopped what they were doing and watched. Just as the elevator doors swished open to take Rebecca to the birthing center, Reverend Jamison said, "Kyle, do you take this woman to be your lawful wedded wife?"

"Yes, I do," Kyle said.

"Rebecca, do you—?"

"I do," she gasped.

"Then I now pronounce you man and wife," Reverend Jamison said, skipping all the rest of the unimportant parts.

Everyone around them cheered.

Rebecca laughed just as another pain hit.

After that, it was all a blur. They got to the birthing center, and Kyle and Lucy came into Rebecca's room with her. Lucy had taken over the role of coach once Rebecca moved to Houston.

Then it was all organized mayhem. The hospital personnel took over, and before Rebecca knew it, she was in her hospital gown and up on the delivery bed and the monitor was hooked up to her stomach. The baby's heartbeat filled the room.

"Mrs. MacNeill?" said one of the nurses.

Rebecca heard nothing else except those wonderful words. Her eyes met Kyle's. He smiled. "I love you, Mrs. MacNeill," he said, bending over to kiss her gently.

"I love you more," Rebecca said.

Lucy grinned.

And at that precise moment, Graham Kyle Mac-Neill decided it was time for him to join the family.

Fifteen minutes later, when the nurse laid her new son in her arms, and Kyle, eyes filled with wonder, touched his finger to the baby's cheek, Rebecca knew that no matter how many wonderful things happened to her in the future, nothing could ever surpass this moment.

* * * * *

Silhouette®

SPECIAL EDITION™

COMING NEXT MONTH

#1075 A LAWMAN FOR KELLY—Myrna Temte
That Special Woman!

U.S. marshal meets gal from the wrong side of the law. Result? Arresting display of sparks until that special woman Kelly Jaynes finally gets her man—handsome lawman Steve Anderson!

#1076 MISTAKEN BRIDE—Brittany Young

Kate Fairfax had always had a troubled relationship with her identical twin. So when her sister asked her to be at her wedding, Kate was happy to attend. But she *never* expected to be so attracted to the groom...or that the upcoming wedding would be her own!

#1077 LIVE-IN MOM—Laurie Paige

Love was in the air the moment Carly Lightfoot and Ty Macklin set eyes on each other. Ty had a ranch and a son to look out for, and didn't have time for romance—that is, until Ty's son decided Carly would make a perfect mom and schemed to get her together with his dad....

#1078 THE LONE RANGER—Sharon De Vita
Silver Creek County

Texas Ranger Cody Kincaid had come to Silver Creek to get the job done—protect widowed Savannah Duncan and her son from someone trying to scare her off her land. But he didn't bargain on getting so attached to the sexy single mom and her mischievous child. Whether Cody knew it or not, this lone ranger needed a family....

#1079 MR. FIX-IT—Jo Ann Algermissen

Finding themselves working side by side was an unexpected bonus for Brandon Corral and Molly Winsome. Her broken heart needed mending, and "Mr. Fix-It" Brandon was sure he was the man for the job....

#1080 ALMOST TO THE ALTAR—Neesa Hart

Elise Christopher and Wil Larson had almost made it to the altar years ago. Now, fate had unexpectedly reunited them, giving them a chance to recapture their romance. But would they make it down the aisle this time?

FAST CASH 4031 DRAW RULES
NO PURCHASE OR OBLIGATION NECESSARY

Fifty prizes of $50 each will be awarded in random drawings to be conducted no later than 3/28/97 from amongst all eligible responses to this prize offer received as of 2/14/97. To enter, follow directions, affix 1st-class postage and mail OR write Fast Cash 4031 on a 3" x 5" card along with your name and address and mail that card to: Harlequin's Fast Cash 4031 Draw, P.O. Box 1395, Buffalo, NY 14240-1395 OR P.O. Box 618, Fort Erie, Ontario L2A 5X3. (Limit: one entry per outer envelope; all entries must be sent via 1st-class mail.) Limit: one prize per household. Odds of winning are determined by the number of eligible responses received. Offer is open only to residents of the U.S. (except Puerto Rico) and Canada and is void wherever prohibited by law. All applicable laws and regulations apply. Any litigation within the province of Quebec respecting the conduct and awarding of a prize in this sweepstakes maybe submitted to the Régie des alcools, des courses et des jeux. In order for a Canadian resident to win a prize, that person will be required to correctly answer a time-limited arithmetical skill-testing question to be administered by mail. Names of winners available after 4/28/97 by sending a self-addressed, stamped envelope to: Fast Cash 4031 Draw Winners, P.O. Box 4200, Blair, NE 68009-4200.

OFFICIAL RULES
MILLION DOLLAR SWEEPSTAKES
NO PURCHASE NECESSARY TO ENTER

1. To enter, follow the directions published. Method of entry may vary. For eligibility, entries must be received no later than March 31, 1998. No liability is assumed for printing errors, lost, late, non-delivered or misdirected entries.

   To determine winners, the sweepstakes numbers assigned to submitted entries will be compared against a list of randomly pre-selected prize winning numbers. In the event all prizes are not claimed via the return of prize winning numbers, random drawings will be held from among all other entries received to award unclaimed prizes.

2. Prize winners will be determined no later than June 30, 1998. Selection of winning numbers and random drawings are under the supervision of D. L. Blair, Inc., an independent judging organization whose decisions are final. Limit: one prize to a family or organization. No substitution will be made for any prize, except as offered. Taxes and duties on all prizes are the sole responsibility of winners. Winners will be notified by mail. Odds of winning are determined by the number of eligible entries distributed and received.

3. Sweepstakes open to residents of the U.S. (except Puerto Rico), Canada and Europe who are 18 years of age or older, except employees and immediate family members of Torstar Corp., D. L. Blair, Inc., their affiliates, subsidiaries, and all other agencies, entities, and persons connected with the use, marketing or conduct of this sweepstakes. All applicable laws and regulations apply. Sweepstakes offer void wherever prohibited by law. Any litigation within the province of Quebec respecting the conduct and awarding of a prize in this sweepstakes must be submitted to the Régie des alcools, des courses et des jeux. In order to win a prize, residents of Canada will be required to correctly answer a time-limited arithmetical skill-testing question to be administered by mail.

4. Winners of major prizes (Grand through Fourth) will be obligated to sign and return an Affidavit of Eligibility and Release of Liability within 30 days of notification. In the event of non-compliance within this time period or if a prize is returned as undeliverable, D. L. Blair, Inc. may at its sole discretion award that prize to an alternate winner. By acceptance of their prize, winners consent to use of their names, photographs or other likeness for purposes of advertising, trade and promotion on behalf of Torstar Corp., its affiliates and subsidiaries, without further compensation unless prohibited by law. Torstar Corp. and D. L. Blair, Inc., their affiliates and subsidiaries are not responsible for errors in printing of sweepstakes and prizewinning numbers. In the event a duplication of a prizewinning number occurs, a random drawing will be held from among all entries received with that prizewinning number to award that prize.

SWP-S12ZD1

5. This sweepstakes is presented by Torstar Corp., its subsidiaries and affiliates in conjunction with book, merchandise and/or product offerings. The number of prizes to be awarded and their value are as follows: Grand Prize — $1,000,000 (payable at $33,333.33 a year for 30 years); First Prize — $50,000; Second Prize — $10,000; Third Prize — $5,000; 3 Fourth Prizes — $1,000 each; 10 Fifth Prizes — $250 each; 1,000 Sixth Prizes — $10 each. Values of all prizes are in U.S. currency. Prizes in each level will be presented in different creative executions, including various currencies, merchandise and travel. Any presentation of a prize level in a currency other than U.S. currency represents an approximate equivalent to the U.S. currency prize for that level, at that time. Prize winners will have the opportunity of selecting any prize offered for that level; however, the actual non U.S. currency equivalent prize, if offered and selected, shall be awarded at the exchange rate existing at 3:00 P.M. New York time on March 31, 1998. A travel prize option, if offered and selected by winner, must be completed within 12 months of selection and is subject to: traveling companion(s) completing and returning a Release of Liability prior to travel; and hotel and flight accommodations availability. For a current list of all prize options offered within prize levels, send a self-addressed, stamped envelope (WA residents need not affix postage) to: MILLION DOLLAR SWEEPSTAKES Prize Options, P.O. Box 4456, Blair, NE 68009-4456, USA.

6. For a list of prize winners (available after July 31, 1998) send a separate, stamped, self-addressed envelope to: MILLION DOLLAR SWEEPSTAKES Winners, P.O. Box 4459, Blair, NE 68009-4459, USA.

EXTRA BONUS PRIZE DRAWING
NO PURCHASE OR OBLIGATION NECESSARY TO ENTER

7. The Extra Bonus Prize will be awarded in a random drawing to be conducted no later than 5/30/98 from among all entries received. To qualify, entries must be received by 3/31/98 and comply with published directions. Prize ($50,000) is valued in U.S. currency. Prize will be presented in different creative expressions, including various currencies, vehicles, merchandise and travel. Any presentation in a currency other than U.S. currency represents an approximate equivalent to the U.S. currency value at that time. Prize winner will have the opportunity of selecting any prize offered in any presentation of the Extra Bonus Prize Drawing; however, the actual non U.S. currency equivalent prize, if offered and selected by winner, shall be awarded at the exchange rate existing at 3:00 P.M. New York time on March 31, 1998. For a current list of prize options offered, send a self-addressed, stamped envelope (WA residents need not affix postage) to: Extra Bonus Prize Options, P.O. Box 4462, Blair, NE 68009-4462, USA. All eligibility requirements and restrictions of the MILLION DOLLAR SWEEPSTAKES apply. Odds of winning are dependent upon number of eligible entries received. No substitution for prize except as offered. For the name of winner (available after 7/31/98), send a self-addressed, stamped envelope to: Extra Bonus Prize Winner, P.O. Box 4463, Blair, NE 68009-4463, USA.

SWP-S12ZD2

As seen on TV!
Free Gift Offer

With a Free Gift proof-of-purchase from any Silhouette® book,
you can receive a beautiful cubic zirconia pendant.

This gorgeous marquise-shaped stone is a genuine cubic
zirconia—accented by an 18" gold tone necklace.

(Approximate retail value $19.95)

Send for yours today...
compliments of 🔷 *Silhouette*®
™

To receive your free gift, a cubic zirconia pendant, send us one original proof-of-
purchase, photocopies not accepted, from the back of any Silhouette Romance™,
Silhouette Desire®, Silhouette Special Edition®, Silhouette Intimate Moments®
or Silhouette Yours Truly™ title available in August, September, October, November and
December at your favorite retail outlet, together with the Free Gift Certificate, plus a
check or money order for $1.65 U.S./$2.15 CAN. (do not send cash) to cover postage and
handling, payable to Silhouette Free Gift Offer. We will send you the specified gift. Allow
6 to 8 weeks for delivery. Offer good until December 31, 1996 or while quantities last.
Offer valid in the U.S. and Canada only.

Free Gift Certificate

Name: _____

Address: _____

City: _____ State/Province: _____ Zip/Postal Code: _____

Mail this certificate, one proof-of-purchase and a check or money order for postage
and handling to: SILHOUETTE FREE GIFT OFFER 1996. In the U.S.: 3010 Walden
Avenue, P.O. Box 9077, Buffalo NY 14269-9077. In Canada: P.O. Box 613, Fort Erie,
Ontario L2Z 5X3.

FREE GIFT OFFER
084-KMD

ONE PROOF-OF-PURCHASE

To collect your fabulous FREE GIFT, a cubic zirconia pendant, you must include this
original proof-of-purchase for each gift with the properly completed Free Gift Certificate.

084-KMD-R

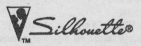